State of the Arts

State of the Arts

Art Shimamura

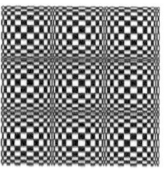

A Beholder Press Publication
Berkeley, CA

ISBN 978-0-578-04767-6

Printed in the United States of America

The author wishes to thank the Children's Hospital Oakland and Brewed Awakenings Café in Berkeley for providing a place to write much of this novel, my parents, Akimitsu and Kazuko Shimamura, for instilling in me a sense of learning and humor, and my immediate family, Helen Ettlinger, Thomas Shimamura, and Gregory Shimamura for providing much of what is important and cherished in my life.

1

"It's art, but so what?" mumbles Professor Shearing to his semi-conscious class of art historian wanna-bes. The title of today's lecture is "The Dissolution of Paint in Minimalism" and even Trudy Jenkins, self-proclaimed star of the class, mindlessly doodles curlicues on her wrist (five years from now, Trudy abandoned graduate school at NYU, shacked up with Boh Ho, a Chinese artist, and was part of his piece entitled "Self-Representation," in which she stood naked in front of Boh's art class reading her unfinished dissertation thesis, which Boh had penned over her entire body. "A fine piece of conceptual art," announced Ben Hera, Boh's effusive instructor). But at this moment, Ted Shearing—known to his students as "Ted the Dead"—lectures as absently as his students listen.

After class, Ted grabs his notes and shuffles down the hall to his office. Head bent, he unlocks the door, sits, and stares intently at his computer screen. He checks his email—no new messages—then jerks the mouse nervously through his internet auctions. In truth, the only excitement that Ted finds these days arrives in the form of anonymous bidders with names like "freakydude" and "hangloose," who are enamored by the same obscure objects d'art as he.

"Damn!" he blurts louder than intended, after losing an auction at the last minute to "slipnslide." With the glumness of failure, Ted slinks from his desk, steps out his office, and readies himself for his daily afternoon routine—lunch with Clare and a ride on an exercise bicycle.

Strolling across the grassy quad of Napa State College, Ted makes his way across campus. He offers only a fleeting glance at the two coeds in skimpy shorts frolicking in the sun, a Frisbee floating between them. The scene is bucolic, though after a decade as a California resident, the state still eludes him.

As he nears the cafeteria, Ted ponders—I'm 35 years old, a tenured professor, and have reached the pinnacle of my existence. If only it were true. Indeed, Ted Shearing, recently tenured professor of Art History, seems to have gone as far as one can in the minor leagues of academia. He asks himself: Why am I so unhappy? Where's my life going?

Ted pulls the heavy glass door of the cafeteria and confronts the hustle and blare within. He finds Clare sitting at a booth focused on her laptop. She looks up, smiles, and says, "Hi!"—then quickly utters, "Hey, what's wrong?" Although Clare Singer is an Associate Professor of Psychology, she didn't need those credentials to appreciate Ted's glumness.

"Nothing really. I'm not sure if it's boredom with my life or my failed attempt to own a Brett Weston in an auction this morning."

"Who's Brett Weston?"

"He's the son of that famous photographer, Edward Weston.

You know, nautilus shells, the nude kneeling with her head down. I almost owned a cool black and white photograph of a cracked windshield."

"Oh," says Clare, sounding less enthusiastic from the photograph's description than she should have. She continues, "Say, I need your opinion, I'm working on an assignment for my writing workshop." Clare, author of numerous research papers and scholarly reviews, fantasizes about life as a famous mystery writer. "I need to put down a profile of a protagonist. I've chosen an academic murder mystery, but I can't decide on a 'Miss Marple' or 'Kinsey Milhone' type. What do you think?"

"How about a Raymond Chandler type with boobs," Ted says, trying unsuccessfully to keep his disposition from seeping into the conversation. "How about 'Samantha Marlowe,' her day job is Professor of Slavic Studies but at night she drinks a half bottle of vodka, scratches her crotch, and solves murders."

Clare smiles, rises to give Ted a passively aggressive smooch, and accepts the fact that he won't be any help. As they walk toward the food counter, she pipes, "Oh, I have some great gossip for you! I found out why Jim Armstrong—you know that crusty prof in my department—why he's been so human lately. It turns out he's having an affair with Cathy, our personnel manager. They were seen necking in his car out at the park yesterday during lunch!"

Somehow this bit of gossip depresses Ted even more. Despite his relationship with Clare, a pert, intelligent, and attractive woman, he wonders why crusty old Jim seems more full of life than he.

"Well," Ted replies, "I guess that's one big step for Jim Armstrong...one small step for mankind."

Ted and Clare have been together for almost three years. Clare, a divorced mother with a 16-year old son, studies animal behavior. Her academic interest helps in parenting, as her son, Kevin, is a beast. Last week, Kevin broke his arm trying to break the local record in skateboard jumping. Ted tolerates Kevin, but admittedly finds the boy much too feral for his liking. Kevin tolerates Ted and considers him the dullard professor that he is. Ted thinks Clare likes him because he's so unlike Kevin. Actually, Clare enjoys Ted's wry sense of humor, intellectual acumen, and adeptness in satisfying her carnal needs.

While standing in the grill line, Clare asks, "What do you want to do this weekend? John has Kevin."

"I dunno, I guess we could hit a museum or check out some galleries in SF or maybe we can just hang out at my place and relax" ('relax' is Ted's private euphemism for engaging in torrid sex).

"Anything is fine with me, we can rent a movie for Saturday night, and I'll fix something, maybe fish?"

"Sure, that sounds great. Say, do you ever feel like you've gone as far in your life as you ever will? I mean, do you sometimes feel like there isn't anything more to do?"

"Whoa, that's heavy, I guess it wasn't just the loss of that Weston thing that's bumming you out." Unfortunately, Clare now realizes that the reminding of that Weston thing, which was snugly out of Ted's consciousness, puts a deeper crease on his brow. "Hey, cheer up, you just got tenure. Now you can spend some quality time working on all those projects you've been wanting to do." Trying further to make amends, Clare continues, "You know, I'm up for a sabbatical too, maybe we could spend a month or two doing research in New York or London?"

"Naw, I dunno." Ted grabs his plate of hamburger and fries from the grill cook. "After writing those two articles in such a rushed way, primarily to get tenure, I'm feeling burnt out."

"Well, then let's take a fun trip and go up north somewhere, maybe hit Mendocino again and just kick back for a few days."

Ted wonders how he came to meet someone like Clare—she's concerned, witty, and likes to relax. Lifting his bun and pouring ketchup over his meat, he answers, "Maybe, I dunno…you know I feel I'm losing direction, I don't know what to do."

"Come on. At least we have fun together, don't we?"

"Yeah, you're incredibly sweet, I'm lucky," admits Ted.

Clare managed to bolster Ted's spirits enough for him to make it to the gym. In front of his locker, Ted stands naked and sucks up his paunch while trying unsuccessfully to stifle a belch, which fills the air with a rush of meat, fries, and ketchup. For his age, Ted looks reasonably fit—achieved primarily from a good set of genes. His pale complexion, unkempt hair, and slightly graying temples mark him clearly in the category of 'non-student'—though in his mind, he identifies more with the "kids" than the faculty.

Now adorned in trunks, t-shirt, and gym shoes, Ted saunters off to the large exercise room. As he enters, his pupils constrict in response to the harsh ceiling lights, which nearly blind him of the row of bright spandex, naked midriffs, and nodding breasts that acknowledge him as he passes by the treadmills. Ted mounts an open bicycle, pushes a few buttons, and sets up his virtual exercise. His routine offers some aerobics, but more importantly, prevention from glum thoughts. He's transfixed on pedaling at a constant 80 rpm, making sure he beats his virtual opponent—a little guy on a bike racing next to his bike, both of which depicted on a small LCD screen attached to the handlebars. Ted always wins, as he sets his opponent to be so slow that there is no real competition.

After his workout, Ted stands underneath a showerhead contemplating his afternoon itinerary. Typically, he would return to his office, check his email, and work on his next lecture (while surfing the web for new art). Today looks to be a typical day. Savoring the warmth of the shower, he wonders if a bid on another auction will be successful. Although less interested in this one than the Brett Weston, Ted still hums with excitement, as he considers the possibility of owning a new work of art. The piece is by an unknown digital video artist and entitled, "Rainbird in Motion." It depicts one those sprinkler heads commonly used on golf courses—the kind that makes that shick, shick, shick sound as it shoots a long spray out its nozzle. "Rainbird in Motion" won a prize and was displayed at a New York gallery (but presumably never sold). The winning bidder receives a DVD disk with a close-up view of a Rainbird as it travels through its rhythmic cycle spraying a semicircle of water then rapidly reversing itself to its starting position. The video includes a continuous loop of the same Rainbird in motion replete with its "shick, shick, shick..." soundtrack. As Ted towels himself, he grins at the concept of "Rainbird" and wonders if he could justify the piece as a tax write-off, as he could use it in his graduate course on art criticism.

The thought of owing Rainbird truly lifts Ted's mood as he leaves the gym. Smiling, he strolls into the administrative offices of the Department of Art and Art History and checks his mail. He finds only book catalogues and the recent issue of *Representations*, which he promptly tosses aside as he enters his office. Correspondences have thinned over the years. In those heady days of graduate school and just after he received his Ph.D., everyone seemed interested in his work. He would receive invitations to conferences and offers from publishers to write scholarly treatises. Now, as a professor in a remote college, no one seems to care. Ted attributes the paucity of mail to the internet, though it occurs to him that even his email correspondences have thinned over the years. Nevertheless, Ted grins, almost giddy with anticipation.

Hunkered down in front of his computer, Ted clicks on his folder of lecture notes. As he opens next week's lecture, he spies a glimpse of his internet browser in the background. He's itching to surf the web and hang ten on that electronic equivalent of Malibu. While he grapples with this intellectual dilemma, Dave Connerly raps on his door so forcefully that the door swings wide and bangs against the wall.

"Hi Teddy boy, how's it hanging?"

"Rather flaccidly, Davey boy."

Dave is the newest member of the department, having just received his Ph.D. from Yale. He studies prehistoric art and is in his pre-jaded period of academic nowhere (i.e., he still receives email). Dave would like nothing more than to be on the faculty at Stanford or NYU, but somehow circumstances, which Dave felt were beyond his control, plunked him down at Napa State. In fact, Napa State was the only place that offered him a job, even though he was interviewed at eight other universities.

"I thought tenure meant spending the afternoons sipping fine wine with intellectuals in little cafes," quips Dave.

"Well, tenure's not all that it's cracked up to be. We all gotta teach."

"Except for the Chair. Hell, we never see Franklin."

Ted considers the remark and wonders what Chairman Franklin, one of the senior members of the department, does during the day. In the past, Franklin spent his afternoons trying to get students to 'relax' with him. However, after a young coed threatened a sexual harassment lawsuit, he cleaned up his act and devoted himself to academic affairs.

Ted replies, "Well, would you want to be the Chair just to hassle with complaints by faculty and students and go to inane meetings with the Dean?"

"Well, at least I wouldn't have to teach to these halfwits. Neanderthals used rocks that were sharper than the students here."

"Speaking of which, I've gotta work on my lecture or else I'll be history."

Taking the hint, Dave saunters off to find someone else to bother.

Ted finds Dave irritating and diametrically opposite to his own demeanor, but nevertheless, he sympathizes. Upon accepting his own position at Napa State, Ted felt slighted, but at least he landed a job. Dave confided similar feelings when he first arrived last year. During their respective first years, they both entertained fantasies about leaving Napa State for bigger and better environs. Yet Ted's attempt to relocate after a year was met with utter disappointment. Not a single interview. It was as if assistant professorship at Napa State was tantamount to leprosy—no one wanted to touch him. Ted figures Dave will experience the same disappointment later this year when he attempts his escape.

Returning to his computer screen, Ted notices that the end of auction is nearing. He suddenly panics, worrying that he might be overbid and lose "Rainbird." Although he currently is the highest bidder, he feels his maximum bid is not high enough. He's afraid that someone will snipe him by bidding higher than his maximum bid at the very last second. With this morning's disappointment and one minute to go, Ted frantically ups his maximum bid, trying to guarantee a win. Even after this quick maneuver, Ted worries that he'll be sniped. He madly clicks and re-clicks his refresh button and watches the seconds creep down—23 seconds, 14 seconds, 9 seconds... Finally, the screen displays "Auction has ended" and his code name, "napart," appears as the winning bidder of "Rainbird in Motion"! Ted blushes, giddy with excitement, though he wasn't sniped. In truth, no one in the entire World Wide Web other than Ted was interested in "Rainbird in Motion."

2

Saturday morning—Ted sits comfortably on his sofa sipping coffee from his mug. He ruffles through the *San Francisco Chronicle*, waiting for Clare to arrive. Ted's big yellow Victorian, with its quaint front porch and bay windows, resembles his childhood home. Ted grew up in Princeton, where his father, now deceased, was a Professor of Computer Science. Life as an only child in a small college town was ordinary and uneventful. Ted's mother dutifully raised him while his father climbed the ladder of big-time academia. As co-inventor of the trash bin icon and the algorithm it uses to delete files, Ted's father sealed his fate both academically and financially. They lived a few blocks from the Princeton campus in the large yellow house, replete with covered porch, swing, and manicured lawn.

When Ted was young, his father invested in various stocks using income garnered from royalties and academic honoraria. Stocks were purchased in Ted's name, and as such, his father favored companies that catered to children, such as Disney and Mattel. Later, when Ted left for college, his father invested in companies that catered to his own needs, such as Pfizer (read Viagra) and Whitehall Robins (read Advil). Thus, when his father died a few years ago, Ted was left with an enormous amount of stock. Even better, Ted escaped the new millennium downturns by diversifying his stock earnings both in the US and abroad. As such, Ted now sits independently wealthy, permitting him the luxury of a full-time professorship at a small college, a substantial art collection, and a life without financial worries, which is entirely unique among professors at Napa State.

When the doorbell rings, Ted moves toward the front door, eager to see Clare. As he approaches, he spies a glimpse of her through the screen door mesh and notices how incredibly fetching she looks. He opens the door, lets her in, and as the door bangs against the house, he runs his eyes over Clare, who is clad in a red "Napa State" t-shirt, the logo curved nicely around her bust, and cut-off jeans, which reveals much of her smooth, tanned thighs. She sports a 49ers cap perched snugly on top with her dark brown ponytail poking out from behind. Ted becomes noticeably aroused; he's pumping for some serious relaxing.

Oblivious to Ted's growing excitement, Clare smiles, "Hi, ready to hit Home Depot?"

"Oh yeah, you wanted to get some washers to fix that leak," Ted answers sullenly as his own hydraulics start to lose pressure.

"Yup, we also need to stop at the fish market and movie place for tonight. Say, maybe you should think about doing some of your own home improvements, maybe brighten up the place with a paint job in the living room."

Ted cringes at the thought. Scanning the room, he knows she's right, but at least the place is cleaned by a housekeeper every week, and anyway his walls are mostly covered with his art collection.

Over the years, with financial help from Disney and Mattel, Ted's collection has grown to over a hundred pieces. Most were bought at West Coast galleries, though his internet purchases have increased considerably. The bulk of Ted's collection collects dust in the closet of his spare bedroom. Indeed, most aren't worth the canvas on which they're impaled. Yet either by luck or artful aesthetics, some of the pieces have dramatically increased in value as the artists who painted them have subsequently passed the Institutional Seal of Approval by the elite guards of what's new and important in the art world.

Of his collection, several stand out. Perhaps his most valuable piece is "Lost Souls #4," by Anita Fleming. Ted bought one of her pieces early on. It hangs over his sofa and consists of a bare canvas onto which an assortment of unpaired shoes, slippers, and boots are glued. Each work in the "Lost Souls" series (there's a total of nine) contains footwear obtained from various lost and found bins. Lost Souls #6 hangs in the New York Museum of Contemporary Art.

Another valuable piece, "Colds and Fevers" by Jonathan Smead, amounts to a bunch of used Kleenex tissues stuck onto a black canvas at various times over a one-year period. Of course, the adhesive is Smead's own nasal mucous. For the protection of the piece (and for Ted's protection), "Colds and Fevers" is encased in a hermetically sealed Plexiglas enclosure, which hangs over Ted's television set. Smead, another accomplished artist, has works in several prestigious galleries across the country. He has been reviewed in *Artforum* and is known for his use of his body as an art supply store. His most famous works to date are "Hair Today" and "Love's Trail." Ted was drawn immediately to "Colds and Fevers" as his first response to the piece was, 'It's Snot Art.'

"What movie do you want to watch tonight?" Clare asks as

Ted drives into the Home Depot parking lot.

"Anything but science fiction."

Though most guys find Home Depot to be a homeowner's wet dream, it's Clare who gets off on the place. In the store, she's quite an anomaly, a slender woman amongst a herd of beer bellies. Ted strolls behind as she walks, almost skipping down the aisle. She's unknowingly turning balding heads, which are closely followed by swinging bellies. Ted conjures up an artistic thought— videotaping the men's responses to Clare as she strolls around the Home Depot. He fantasizes that it would make for an interesting video art piece.

Clare collects her plumbing supplies, and as she strolls past the hot tubs, she turns to Ted and says, "Hey big boy, why don't you put one of those in your house? It'd be great fun sloshing around."

Ted's imagination runs rampant. "You got it! We can remodel the entire bathroom. I've always wanted a nice soaking tub, maybe add a sound system and of course bookshelves for my bathroom reading."

"Yeah, you could sell the Smead and pay for the entire remodel."

"But it's snot art!" chides Ted, which Clare understands cannot be forgotten when it comes to discussions about "Colds and Fevers."

"I'm still amazed that that thing hanging over your TV is, what did you say, worth over 50 grand."

"Probably more now," says Ted, "I just read that a Smead was purchased by the Guggenheim."

Driving back to Ted's house, Clare recalls, "Oh yeah, did you hear about that art guy in London who got fired because he said conceptual art was trash?"

"Yeah, we were all talking about it the other day after our faculty meeting. Everyone was asking me about it." Ted continues, "It appears that this fellow was released from his position as director of an art institute because he said that conceptual art was dead. Not a good vocational ploy. He certainly had guts, considering how entrenched he was in the art world. I suggested that rather than spouting off like that, he should have written a satiric commentary about the lack of substance in contemporary art."

"Well, good thing we have tenure. It's amazing that someone would get fired just because of some critical remarks."

"Yeah, it's hard to imagine what we could do to get fired from our jobs," says Ted.

Even in high school, Ted thought that academia would make for a cushy job. His interest was guided by watching his father, who, despite working long hours, was able to do things that other fathers weren't able to do, such as pick him up after school, spend summers at home, and take trips all over the world. When it was time to apply for college, Ted already had an academic career in mind. He hoped to escape his small, college town existence and searched the continent for a city that bustled in modernity. But alas, New York was too hectic, Los Angeles too tacky, and Seattle too moldy. So, Ted settled for a liberal arts education at Williams College—the prototypical small, college town. His college life consisted of majoring in History, losing his virginity, and graduating cum laude.

The process of applying to graduate school landed Ted in Berkeley, where he earned his Ph.D. in Art History. Battling against the wave of postmodern, deconstructive criticism, Ted combined his genetic predisposition toward computers with his avocational interest in movies. He developed a doctoral thesis on the portrayal of computers in film. As such, Ted wasted most of his graduate school days watching bad science fiction and digitizing video clips of nearly every computer portrayed in the movies up to 2000. Ted's aversion to science fiction now matches his sentiment toward postmodern theory.

When they reach the front porch, Ted opens the screen door for Clare, and as it slams back, Ted's adrenal output enters overdrive and his lower hydraulics begin to rise to the occasion. Had Clare been aware of Ted's arousal when she arrived in the morning, she could have told him that his current state was caused by a conditioned response to the sound of the door slamming (i.e., the conditioned stimulus) that was paired earlier with the presence of Clare's supple body (i.e., the unconditioned stimuli), and just like Pavlov's dog, Ted is salivating, as he moves toward the unconditioned stimuli. Clare, now aware of Ted's behavioral response, gives him a lascivious grin and signals with her eyebrows to come and get it. As the stimulus and response are about to meet, Clare's cell phone elicits the ominous ringtone of Darth Vader's leitmotif.

Clare grabs her phone and says, "Hi John, what's up...What!"

After a few un-huh's, Clare says, "Shit. I'll be right over."

Clare hangs up, turns to Ted and says, "John just got a call from the Santa Rosa Police. Kevin got hauled in along with some friends for trying to set off a small bomb at a 7-11 parking lot. I need to pick him up and bring him home."

"We can take my car," says Ted.

"No it's OK, it's an hour's drive, and I gotta deal with Kevin—and John—about this. You stay here and relax."

"OK," says Ted, realizing that relaxing is not what he's going to get this weekend.

Clare grabs her purse, kisses goodbye, and quickly pulls out of the driveway, leaving Ted with some raw salmon and "Pulp Fiction."

3

Monday morning—"I hope you all had a relaxing weekend," Ted greets his class, feeling the sting of irony.

"Today's lecture is on the 'Psychology of Representation.' What do I mean by that? Well..." Ted begins his favorite lecture. It's the only one that has his students oohing and ahhing. He shows cute visual illusions lifted directly from one of Clare's Psychology 1 lectures.

Ted asks his attentive class, "Now, how many of you have been to the 'Mystery Spot' near Santa Cruz?"

"I have!" blurts Trudy raising her hand at the same time. "Me and my boyfriend went last summer. It's really cool. Like some weird gravitational vorpex or something. It makes people shrink and grow, trees grow crooked and balls roll uphill and all sorts of weird things like that."

"Yeah, it's truly a strange place." says Ted. "Check this out..." Ted shows a slide of two people standing in "The Mystery Spot"—in actuality in front of a tilted shed that is resting against a hillside. The shed looks as if it witnessed a major earthquake at close range.

He then shows another slide in which the same two people have switched positions, and it looks as if one has shrunk and the other has grown.

"That's totally weird!" exclaims Rick Seitz, wide-eyed and alert, which is not his usual demeanor. Rick attends class fully stoned, reeking of his special cologne, *eau de bong*, though his medication apparently has not fully kicked in yet.

Ted continues, "Well, it turns out that what you might think is some gravitational vortex or some other strange physical anomaly is really all in your head. It's just a visual illusion. In fact, two Berkeley psychologists did some experiments on this illusion and you can show it anywhere. The trick is in the tilted shed. Our mind tries to straighten the tilt and make the shed upright and normal. When we do this, the height of the two people gets distorted. You all should go to the Mystery Spot, it's a fun place."

"That is so totally weird!" murmurs Rick, as his medication kicks in.

Ted's on a roll. "You see, these illusions tell us that what we see is not exactly what's out there in reality. Our mind interprets the world. In psychological terminology, we *represent* the world, it's not a direct copy."

"That's cool," says Mike Gallegos, "but I already heard all of this stuff last semester in Dr. Singer's Psych 1 class. What does this have to do with art?"

"Good question, Mike." Ted begins to feel a bit guilty by the revelation of his plagiarism. "Well, you see, art nowadays attempts to reveal the nature of representation. What I mean is that contemporary artists don't try to copy the real world. Instead, they try to highlight the ways in which the medium—paint, canvas, lines—has been used as symbols or representations of art."

Ted is losing them. Like a fading TV signal, the class appears vague and diffuse. Fortunately, the illusions take up most of the time and the end of class arrives. As the students disperse, Ted packs up and relives the momentary exuberance he felt when he held their attention. He considers writing a paper on the psychology of modernist art, perhaps with Clare's help. Walking out the building toward the cafeteria, he considers the link between psychology and modern art and how it may offer a new direction in his scholarly activities.

"I can't believe it," says Clare, watching Ted dunk a French fry into a pool of ketchup. "Kevin and his buddies actually tried to set a bomb off at a 7-11."

With mouth full, Ted asks, "How'd they make the bomb?"

"They concocted a kind of Molotov cocktail. They filled a wine bottle with gasoline, stuffed a rag into its neck and, get this, they stuffed a firecracker into the rag, you know, one of those little red ones they sell in Chinatown. The policeman said it would have been serious had they managed to set it off."

"Yeah, with those gas fumes, the thing probably would have exploded in their faces when they tried to light it," Ted remarks, impressed by such insanity.

"That's what the policeman said, too. The store manager knew something was up when he saw the bottle with the rag, so he immediately called the police. Before the kids could light the thing, the police drove up and did the full 'Cops' show arrest."

"Wow, how did Kevin deal with that?"

"He was terrified. He said a policeman shoved him against the patrol car, forced his hands behind his back, which was doubly painful because of his broken arm, and handcuffed him. When I got to the station all of the other parents were there and talking to the policeman, who was gruff but considerate, as it was a first-time offense for all of the boys. Kevin was so freaked out by the whole incident that on the way home he kept on apologizing. Since the incident he's been a saint."

"Well at least sainthood didn't come posthumously. Where was John during all this excitement?"

"He was at his house working, or playing, on his computer. I can't believe that he would dump Kevin with friends during the occasional weekends when he has custody. He could at least spend a little quality time with him."

With his fries gone and Clare's tale deteriorating into wrathful complaints about her ex-husband, Ted feels it's time to head off. On the way to the gym, he considers Kevin's foray into explosives. He fondly recollects an incident in which he and a friend crumpled newspaper into a coffee can, lit the newspaper with matches, and then tossed several rolls of caps into the flames. From a safe distance they waited for a healthy explosion, but nothing happened. Disappointed, they approached the can, confused as to why their mission had failed. Just as they both leaned in to peer, a healthy explosion erupted spraying them with smoke and ashes and leaving them temporarily deaf. Ted's memory of this event softens his feelings for Kevin. It gives Ted confidence that Kevin might not grow up to be an anarchist or mush-brained vegetable.

Pedaling on the exercise bicycle, Ted pants more heavily than usual, unable to rid himself of the uncanny similarity between Kevin's event and his own childhood experience. He considers the satisfaction and fascination of explosives. Suddenly, an idea pops into mind—explosives in performance art. This thought so invades Ted's consciousness that he stops pedaling in the middle of his workout. As he is overtaken by the little bicyclist on the LCD screen, he envisions a brilliant demonstration for his upcoming lecture.

In the shower, Ted presumes that someone must already have used explosives in some work of art. As steam rises off his body, he wonders—has anyone tried to blow up art itself? Quickly, Ted towels himself, puts on clothes, and rather than going back to his office, he heads toward his car. It's 2 o'clock, and as he opens his car door, he thinks he may be able to make it to Chinatown and back before rush hour.

Zooming down Highway 101, Ted formulates his plan. He'll need to visit Chinatown first and get some firecrackers. Then, on the way home, he'll stop at Home Depot for some other stuff—rags, a gas can, and maybe a large trashcan. As he imagines his set-up, Ted notices the fog swirling around the top of the Golden Gate Bridge. Visibility, however, is clear enough to see that the cars are already piling up on the other side. It looks like the return home will be a slow one.

Ted loves the drive through San Francisco. He cuts across Golden Gate Park on his way. It takes a little longer, but it's much prettier. In fact, the rolling fog and greenery reminds him of earlier days in graduate school when he made frequent visits to the SF museums and art galleries. As he enters downtown, Ted realizes that parking will be difficult around Chinatown. He drives further south and locates an open spot just off Mission Street, a few blocks from the Museum of Modern Art. He pushes quarters into the meter, figuring that the stroll through the financial district and up the hill will do him some good, as he didn't finish his workout at the gym.

Rounding the corner just past the Museum, Ted approaches

one of his favorite galleries—the Hugh Gray Gallery. He slows and watches a display in the window. It's a white TV/DVD combo showing a woman sitting on a rumpled bed and sobbing. Suddenly, the image shifts to an "I Love Lucy" episode in which Lucy cries over something Desi has said. A few seconds later, the image cuts back to the same woman as before, only she's on a swing in a playground, laughing as she extends her legs forward, reaching the top of her flight then tucking her legs back as she swings in reverse. Intrigued by the video, Ted enters the gallery to get a closer look. When he reaches the display, a thin, well-dressed fellow greets him.

"Hello, Ted, long time, no see."

"Hi Hugh. I was just on my way to Chinatown, and I noticed this interesting video. What is it?"

"I got it last week. It's called 'I Loved Lucy.' It's by an artist named Tom Cameron. He videotaped his girlfriend, Lucy, during their entire two-year relationship. He was a fanatic, capturing all facets, from their first meeting to their last fight. He had his whole house wired with video cams. This work includes over 200 clips of his girlfriend spliced between clips from the 'I Love Lucy' show. It's over three hours long. Cameron has some other video art pieces. A few of them sold rather handsomely in New York last year. I got this one because he wanted to have some representation in San Francisco. CONART might want to display it next month if it doesn't get sold by then."

"Interesting" Ted realizes it's just the kind of thing the SF Museum of Contemporary Art, known in the art world as SF CONART, would want. Ted finds the piece intriguing as it juxtaposes the poignancy of real life with the superficiality of a sitcom. "What's the piece go for?"

"It's $12,000, which is pretty good, since his earlier work is now up to around twenty grand."

"It's neat, I'll think about it. I gotta go now. How late are you open today?"

"We close at 5, but I'll be in the back room 'til 6. If you want, just ring the bell, I'll come out."

"OK. See ya."

Ted leaves the gallery and makes his way up through the financial district. It amazes him how exceedingly well manicured everyone looks. The men sport dark suits, some revealing slick pinstriped vests underneath. Most carry attaché cases and chat on cell phones or flirt with women who look dressed for advancement. Ted—adorned in jeans, plaid cotton shirt, and nylon jacket—looks like he's from a different planet, or at least a different class bracket. He talks himself into smugness, wanting to let everyone know that he's a tenured professor and doesn't need to dress up for work. Yet he can't get over the feeling that those passing by maintain a wide berth, worried that they might contract some weird rural disease.

As he climbs up Stockton St. and enters Chinatown, the clientele changes dramatically. The sidewalk bustles with Asians of all ages in all sorts of attire. Tourists crowd the street, moving from one souvenir shop to another, even though all of them appear to sell the same colorful junk. Ted feels awkward, never having shopped for explosives. He enters a souvenir shop and approaches an elderly man sitting behind the counter, "Do you know where I can purchase some firecrackers?"

"What?" says the fellow in a thick Chinese accent.

"Do you have any firecrackers?"

"What? Rice crackers?"

"No, firecrackers, you know Fourth of July, little red things with fuse." Ted tries to pantomime a little red thing that goes boom.

"What? Firecrackers...no we no got," says the fellow, relieved that the conversation is over.

"Do you happen to know where I could buy some?"

"What?" The fellow is quite annoyed, as it was clear that the conversation was over.

Slowly, pausing between each word, Ted asks, "Where can I buy some?"

"Ling's up street. Go back of store." The fellow now turns to the elderly woman sitting next to him and converses in rapid Chinese, as if to say more clearly than he could in English that his conversation with Ted is definitely over.

When Ted reaches Ling's, he realizes that there are differences between souvenir shops. Ling's has the ambiance of an upscale gift store that was bustling sometime during the gold rush. Now it appears dark and colorless, and all the tourists are passing around the doorway, as if worried that they might contract some ancient rural disease. Ted maneuvers around narrow aisles stuffed with musty, old, even used-looking products. Dust covers everything, and the shop smells of age and faraway lands. Piled up against the wall are tattered cardboard boxes with faded Chinese characters printed on them. Peeking out of an opening between two boxes, an old torn poster advertises a cheesy Chinese martial arts movie. It's eerie and completely foreign. With every step toward the back, Ted feels as if he's moving away from the here and now. He imagines Rod Serling standing in the corner, smoking a cigarette, about to utter his pronouncement: "Consider if you will, Ted Shearing, mild mannered professor who just walked into Ling's Souvenir Shop hoping to buy some firecrackers. What Ted doesn't realize, is that he's just stepped into...the Twilight Zone."

When he reaches the rear counter, a clatter of wooden beads signals the arrival of a young Asian man, who has just come through an opening to a back room. The entryway is draped with stringed wooden beads of various colors and sizes. The fellow, dressed completely in black—black slacks, dress shirt, jacket and tie—says, with perfect, almost British articulation, "May I help you?"

"I'm looking for firecrackers."

The man glares at Ted and says, "Do you realize that the detonation of fireworks is illegal in the city and in most counties around San Francisco?"

"Oh. Well, I was hoping to buy some for a class demonstration. You see, I'm a professor at Napa State College."

A bit more animated, the fellow says, "I have friends who went to Napa. Let me check the back room. We may have some left over from last year."

As Ted waits, he encounters a wave of guilt as his plan now calls for the purchase of illicit goods. Beads of sweat glisten on his forehead, and just when he's about to bag the whole thing, the clatter of beads signals the reappearance of the salesman.

"I found one package of Red Devils in the back. They're from last year's stock, so I cannot guarantee that they will even work. If you want them, I can sell them to you for fifteen dollars."

"OK," says Ted, surprised by his own voice uttering the affirmation.

Ted hands the fellow a twenty dollar bill, receives his change and a bag with five little red things that are supposed to go boom.

4

Tuesday morning—Ted sits, sipping his morning coffee and watching "I Loved Lucy." Impulse buying put this new artwork on the kitchen table. The screen is pitch dark, though the sounds of grunting and bed squeaking reveal the nature of the action. The sounds, however, are more mechanical than erotic, and Ted wonders if he and Clare sound so dispassionate when they're making love. The video suddenly shifts to an "I Love Lucy" scene in which Lucy, working at a candy factory as a quality control inspector, frantically stuffs chocolates in her mouth as the candy moves down a conveyor belt. After ten seconds of this, the screen darkens completely, and Lucy moans softly and murmurs, "there...there...a little harder...ooh yeah." Ted perks up while Lucy continues, "Now go down...more...there, that's the spot...oh God...okay, now other shoulder blade, that's it....scratch a little harder."

Ted finishes his coffee and turns the Lucys off. He saunters to the living room, sits on the sofa, and admires the "art" supplies in front of him. There's a large aluminum trashcan, a gasoline can filled with unleaded regular, a funnel, some rags, an empty wine bottle, and his package of Red Devils. The critical question now is what lucky piece will be the first object d'annihiliation. Ted rejects "I Loved Lucy" as it's too new for him to consider. As he mentally flips through his collection, his eyes glance above the television to the Plexiglas case that contains "Colds and Fevers." Ted ponders while staring at the work. A brilliant thought erupts. He can use the case itself for his Molotov cocktail and dispense with the wine bottle.

With a sinister grin, Ted scampers to his hall closet and rummages through boxes, throwing stuff aside in search of his cordless drill. His eyes widen when he locates it, then elicits an evil grin when he squeezes the trigger and admires the grinding whirr of the gears. Back in the living room, Ted reaches over to the Smead, and, with his free hand, yanks the thing off the wall. He does this so forcefully that the tissues inside quiver in response. He sets the piece on the floor and goes back to the closet to retrieve his drill bits. He screws the largest bit onto the drill and proceeds to stab holes into the top of the Plexiglas case. After several punctures, Ted manages to make a rough oval opening. He pauses, as a drop of sweat moves from his cheek to the carpet.

Normally Ted would be at his office, working on his next lecture. Disregarding a sense of employment, he stays at home to finish his art project. He figures he'll perform his first act tomorrow in his Introduction to Modern Art class. As such, he won't have to do much preparation for the class. Indeed, with five Red Devils, he can substitute a week's worth of lectures with performance art. Rather than criticizing contemporary art, he'll blow it to pieces.

Looking at his watch, Ted picks up his phone and dials Clare's office, "Hey, I have an idea, how about I pick you up for lunch today. Instead of eating at the cafeteria we'll go out somewhere."

"Sounds like fun, but I have to be back by 1:30 for a meeting."

"No problem. How about I meet you in front of the Psych Building at noon?"

"OK, but why the fancy lunch?"

"Well, I kinda want to surprise you." Just as Ted says this, he realizes that Clare might think it has something to do with their relationship. He clarifies, "I want to tell you about an art project I have in mind."

"Cool."

"OK, I'll see you in a while. Bye."

With some time to kill, Ted kneels on the carpet and continues working on his project. He picks up the cellophane package of firecrackers and tries to tear open the wrapping. When he fails, he sticks a corner of it in his mouth, bites down, and pulls. He succeeds all too well, as half the wrapper rips opens, scattering the little Red Devils on the carpet. He picks one up and carefully rolls it in the rag, making sure that the fuse is exposed. He grabs the Smead and tries to stuff the rag with the Red Devil into the rough oval opening. The opening, however, is not quite large enough. He unrolls the rag, letting the Red Devil drop, and tries to tear the rag in half. When he fails, he sticks a corner of it in his mouth, bites down, and pulls hard. This time, nothing happens except that he nearly pulls out his incisors.

With rag in hand, Ted gets up and walks to the study. He grabs a pair of scissors, cuts a small slit into the rag, and then savagely rips the rag in half with his hands. Returning to the living room, he retrieves a Red Devil and once again rolls it into the rag. This time the rag and firecracker fit snugly into the hole and looks rather impressive. For tomorrow, prior to detonation Ted will unplug the hole and use the funnel to pour gasoline into the Plexiglas case.

Ted puts the drill and bits back into the closet. In the corner, he notices his camera bag. When Ted was a boy, his father gave him a Nikon camera with several lenses. In high school, he took a photography class. He even set up his own darkroom in a spare bathroom, though he didn't really get past cliché images of sunsets, flowers, and barns. After high school, Ted lost interest. Now, he owns a digital camera—a rather expensive one—that he uses for snapshots during vacations. In the interest of documenting his project, Ted slings the camera bag over his shoulder and goes back to the living room. He snatches the Smead, the rag and fuse still sticking out the top, and places it on the kitchen table, propped up against the white TV/DVD combo in which the two Lucys cohabitate. Ted grabs his camera and takes a snap to document the creation of "Molotov Smead."

At noon, Ted finds his keys, locks up, and hustles out to his car. Reaching the campus, he swings into the lot near the Psychology Building and sees Clare by the door chatting with some students. Seeing Ted approach, Clare politely ends her conversation and walks toward the curb. Even though Clare doesn't dress like her students, she looks exuberantly youthful. Smiling, she opens the car door, sits down, says "Hiya," and squeezes Ted's thigh.

"Hi," says Ted, reciprocating the greeting by massaging Clare's thigh, though quite a bit higher than Clare's squeeze.

"Hey, big boy, we certainly are frisky today. So, where do you wanna eat?"

"I thought we'd go into town and hit *The Elegant Cave*." This is Ted's favorite restaurant. It's dark, quiet, and one of the few places that serves both great wine and great grease. The owner, Harry Burns, prides himself as the best barbeque cook in Napa Valley. An extraordinary wine connoisseur, Harry also boasts the largest cellar in town. Having been to France many times, Harry wanted his restaurant to express his combined zeal for BBQ cooking and those quaint *wine caves* where Parisians hang around and sip wine. Thus, *The Elegant Cave* is decorated in Late Paleolithic tones—the room is illuminated with candles and has fake rock walls covered with primitive drawings of horses and bison. With the addition of white tablecloths and finely carved furniture, Harry gives the feel of eating elegantly with Neanderthals in Lascaux.

After ordering, Ted reveals the nature of this special event. "Actually I have to thank Kevin for giving me the inspiration."

"What are you talking about?" says Clare, completely confused.

"Well, that incident in Santa Rosa, I started thinking about a conceptual art project in which I would blow up art."

"Wait a minute, what are you thinking? Are you going to throw a Molotov cocktail in SF MOMA?"

"Definitely not. There's some great art in there. No I'm thinking of blowing up my own collection."

"You've got to be joking."

"No, really," says Ted, as the waiter sets a Fred Flintstone-sized rack of ribs in front of him and an equally large portion of BBQ chicken in front of Clare. Their plates are so full that the waiter delivers a stack of steak fries on a separate plate.

Ted grabs a rib and digs in. After a moment, he swallows and says, "I actually went to Chinatown yesterday and bought some firecrackers. I also got stuff at Home Depot to make a Molotov cocktail. Then today I had this amazing idea. Instead of making a bomb to blow up an art piece, I thought I could make a Molotov cocktail out of the art piece itself. My first victim is going to be

'Colds and Fevers'."

"Right," says Clare, "because it's snot art," managing to beat Ted to the punch.

"I drilled a hole on top of the case and stuck a rag and firecracker into it. Tomorrow during class, I'll put some gas into the case and blow the thing up!"

With a deathly serious stare, Clare says, "Ted, are you totally out of your mind? You, and God forbid, one of your students might get hurt, not to mention how much that piece is worth."

Ted says calmly, "No, I've thought about that. I bought an aluminum trashcan at the Home Depot and will do the whole thing in the can with the lid closed and with all of us at a safe distance. We can still get that hot tub; I can easily sell some other stuff that I have."

"Where do you think you're going to perform this insane act?"

"I figured I'd take the class out to the Quad and do it."

"You're really serious about this, aren't you?"

"Well, at first I didn't know if I was just kidding myself, but after getting the firecrackers, I figured it would be a great way to express my own feelings about contemporary art. This might be the most creative thing I've ever done!"

Clare, still in disbelief, hasn't touched her food. Ted, on the other hand, has his fingers covered with grease and is nearly done with his brontosaurus. Moreover, he has eaten all of the fries, not to mention downing more than a half a bottle of a very good merlot (and half a bottle of ketchup with his fries).

"Well, I don't know what to say," says Clare. Even with her knowledge of abnormal psychology, she cannot think of anything that might dislodge Ted from this crazy idea.

"Well, if you're free around 11:30, you might come by the

Quad."

"Are you kidding? I don't even want to be on campus. You could be risking your job doing this," says Clare in dark tones.

"Do you think so? I've got tenure."

"But you know the idea of tenure has to do with what you can say in class and how you express yourself in your work. It doesn't cover explosions on campus."

"I don't think they can fire me for this," Ted says without confidence. A little more emphatically he states, "Anyway, this is how I'm expressing my feelings about contemporary art."

"Well, I don't think the Dean will be very happy about your method of art criticism. If word gets out, it could make Napa State the laughing stock of academia."

"Well, let's face it, it sort of already is. I imagine that no one will even notice."

"I hope you're right. Things have been so peaceful, so fun, lately. I was just thinking about how comfortable our relationship has been."

"Yeah, I feel the same way, but you know, I've become so antsy, even depressed, about life. As much as I enjoy being with you, my own future seems bleak. I don't think I've ever been this excited about my work in my entire life!"

Ted's excitement matches Clare's disappointment. He watches as Clare pick at her food and realizes the impact this project has on her. He tries to reconcile, "You know, your feeling about this tells me you really care, and I love you for that. If I weren't feeling so damned bummed about my work, I'd probably think this act is as crazy as you think, but lately I've been feeling so...so lacking in purpose and substance. Maybe I'll get fired for this, but hey, I can always live off my investments. Worst comes to worst, we get married, and I'll be your househusband and bring you your slippers every evening and ask you how your day at work has been."

That comment brings a slight smile to Clare. She says, "Great. You and Kevin can spend the weekends together in the backyard making explosives. We'll call it bonding with bombs."

Clare's joke permits an uncomfortable truce. As they exit the Cave, the afternoon sun is blinding. Squinting, they head for the car and back to campus. Ted brakes in front of the Psychology Building and gives Clare a loving kiss, which is affectionately reciprocated.

Home again, Ted sits in front of his computer staring at the screen. His study contains the newest in high-tech equipment. With a top-flight scanner he digitizes art images from books for his courses. An expensive printer produces photographic quality prints. His high-speed internet connection enables him to cruise the internet highway in the fast lane.

Preparing for his lecture, Ted searches the web with the phrase, "conceptual art." The computer spits back the top 100 websites and indicates the facility to regurgitate an additional 3,950,000 others on demand. Scrolling down the list, Ted encounters *www.virtualconart.org*—one of the hottest contemporary art websites. The site showcases new art from around the world. Featured artists are selected by a group of New York insiders, and the site claims that only the best of the best and the newest of the new are displayed. Most of the artists are unknown, presumably fresh upstarts.

As Ted surveys the site, he's convinced that contemporary art has lost its heart (and acquired much too much brain). Much of what is shown looks like derivations of past works by Picasso, Matisse, Warhol, or Duchamp. As he clicks around, he finds links to *Sense Art*, *Thought Art*, *Word Art*, and *Memory Art*. Ted enters *Sense*

Art, and gets another menu—*Sound Art, Smell Art, Taste Art, Felt Art*. Of course, "visual art" is conspicuously absent.

In the *Smell Art* section, Ted finds descriptions of several installations. The first is called, "New Mown Lawn," in which the artist, Chip Devitt from Kentucky, pushes an old-fashioned lawn mower in a large gallery at the Louisville Museum of Modern Art. The floor appears covered with grass, though upon closer inspection an attractive gold frame surrounds the lawn. Ted watches a video clip in which Chip pushes the mower back and forth across the lawn, without a grass catcher, so that the clippings fly around him, presumably permeating the room with that familiar summer scent. Of course, Chip mows the lawn in the nude, one of the requisites of performance art. Expecting the worst, Ted foregoes "It's My Potty" and "Jim's Gym Bags," the other two Smell Art installations.

Ted realizes that the entire site is nonsense, including "Sense Art." He shuts off his computer, satisfied that over the years little of importance or innovation has occurred in contemporary art. In fact, he is buoyed by the notion that Molotov Smead exceeds anything he's seen on the web. With that comfort in mind, Ted settles down to a quiet evening.

5

Wednesday morning—Shick, shick, shick... Ted drives into the campus lot as a flock of Rainbirds spray the Quad. It's early and the lot is completely empty. Ted parks and admires the serene view, until suddenly he's sprayed by an over-enthusiastic Rainbird. Under the cover of a drenched windshield, he sits quietly in his cocoon sipping a café latte. On the drive over, Ted ate most of a currant scone he bought at the bake shop, the remaining bits scattered like a comet's tail between the passenger seat and his lap. Ted ponders today's event and feels an odd sense of awakening, almost sexual in nature, as Molotov Smead reclines quietly in the back seat.

After several pummelings by the Rainbird, the shicking stops, and Ted emerges from his dripping car. Full of caffeine and ready to start the day, he leaves Smead behind and strolls to his office, still experiencing an odd, titillating sensation. As he scans his desk, he notices the little red light blinking on his answering machine. Ted punches the message button.

"Hi love, it's me. I'm not going be around for lunch today. I'm too nervous about what's going to happen to you at the Quad. I'm going to stay home and work this morning. I'll be back in the afternoon. Why don't you come over for dinner tonight and you can fill Kevin and me in on the day's event. Come over any time after 5:30, we'll eat around 6:30. Love you...I'm afraid, but I hope things work out for you. Call me if you need me."

Ted feels abandoned by Clare but understands, as a small part of him also feels like being somewhere else. He peers at his computer screen, which is egging him on for some early morning surfing. Too excited to sit, he leaves the office, and heads down the hall to the classroom. He grabs a stubby piece of chalk and writes, "Professor Shearing's Class will meet at the Quad today." With an hour before show time, Ted heads to the Quad to set up.

When the bell tower chimes the hour, Ted stands and says to his students, "We've talked about conceptual art and its reaction against traditional art, which is best represented as a painting on canvas attractively framed and hanging in an art museum."

Ted has to yell, as he doesn't have the usual acoustics of the classroom. Some students are standing while most sit on the concrete planter that borders the Quad. Ted is giddy with anticipation, though his shoes are wet and covered with blades of grass. The trashcan sits about 50 feet behind him near the middle of the grassy Quad. Molotov Smead leans languidly against the trashcan. The piece of rag and a Red Devil are tucked snugly in Ted's pants pocket.

Ted continues, "Today we're out here, because I want to demonstrate several things about contemporary art. First, I want you all to see a work of art, actually two works. The first is a piece by a relatively famous artist named Jonathan Smead." Ted walks over to the piece, picks it up, and shows it to the students. He walks slowly in front of them so that each has a chance to peruse the piece. He does this in much the same way a kindergarten teacher would show a picture in a storybook or the way a magician would show that his box is empty, saying "...and there's nothing up my sleeves."

"You might wonder what's going on with this artwork. Well, you can see inside the case that the canvas has Kleenex tissues of various colors stuck on it. I'll give you a hint. This work is called 'Colds and Fevers.'"

"Yuck!" screams Trudy. Others are giggling.

"Yes, Trudy, you are correct. It's snot art." The joke bombs; no one gets it. "I mean, for a year Smead stuck used tissues on his canvas every time he had a cold...or fever."

"Ha. I get it, it's snot art. Pretty good Professor Shearing," says Mike Gallegos.

"That's really gross. Why would anyone do such a gross thing?" pipes Trudy.

"Well, believe it or not, this piece and others in which Smead uses his own body as material for his artwork are quite famous in the contemporary art world. Can anyone tell me what's going on here?"

Mike takes a stab, "I think this piece is totally stupid, but one could claim that the artist is making a statement about the human struggle of artistic expression and the social ramifications of personal sacrifice in art."

"That's good, Mike. I couldn't have said it better myself."

Mike grins and prides himself on his descriptive ability. He's a staff reporter for the *Napa State Daily*, the campus newspaper which is affectionately called the *Daily Nap*.

Trudy, not to be outdone, says, "But it's so gross, it's really gross."

"I couldn't agree with you more, though I should tell you that I own this piece. Anyway, I told you that 'Colds and Fevers' is not the only artwork that I will show you today. I'm also going to contrast this more traditional work of art with performance art. Now with performance art there doesn't have to be a canvas, paint, or even an object to show. Most importantly, unlike traditional works of art, performance art happens. It is not meant to last." Ted leaves out the point that many artists perform in the nude, as he certainly will not disrobe for art's sake.

The students are befuddled but attentive. No one can figure out what Ted has up his sleeves.

Ted continues, "Now in addition to demonstrating my own work in the realm of performance art, I also want you to know that my work represents a form of art criticism. That is, I'm going to make a commentary about what I think about contemporary art."

The students are more befuddled and less attentive. They perk up, however, as Ted slips a Red Devil out of his pocket and dangles it in front of the class.

"You see this thing? This is part of my artwork." Half the students are extremely excited (mostly males) and the other half are extremely nervous (mostly females).

"That's totally cool!" exclaims Rick Seitz, the village pothead. "A real firecracker!"

The students watch Ted stick the Red Devil back into his pocket and walk to the trashcan. He reaches into the trashcan and lifts outs a can of gasoline. Ted is far enough away from the students that he can barely hear anything that they're saying. It's as if he's in his own invisible, soundproof bubble. Instead of yelling from this distance, he lifts the Plexiglas case and points to the top of it to show the students the opening that he made. He then reaches into the trashcan once again and retrieves a funnel. As in any good performance, Ted raises the funnel so all can see. He inserts the funnel into the hole, uncaps the gas can, and pours some gasoline into the Plexiglas frame. The tissues soak up some gasoline, while the rest trickles down the sides. Ted grabs the rag and firecracker from his pocket, and as before at home, he rolls them up and stuffs them into the hole.

Ted pours more gas into the trashcan, props Molotov Smead against the trashcan, and trots back to the students.

"Are you really gonna blow the thing up?" asks Rick.

"Yeah, but as they say on TV, 'Don't try this at home'."

"Is that kinda of a Molotov cocktail?" asks Mike.

"Yes, but you can see I've added the firecracker, so we should get a nice bang out of it."

"Is this legal? Does the Dean know about this?" asks Trudy.

"I don't know if it's legal to ignite a firecracker on campus but the artwork is mine, so I can do anything I want with it. As for the authorities, I haven't told them but I don't really care about that," answers Ted.

The statement satisfies Trudy, and for the first time, she gets a moist little tingle as she fantasizes about having sex with Professor Shearing. Trudy has a thing for bad boys.

Ted announces, "I call my work, 'Molotov Smead.' What I'm gonna do is toss a match in the trashcan, which will ignite the gas fumes. Then, I'll put Smead into the flames. With the lid closed and at this safe distance, the firecracker and gas will blow the piece up, thus fulfilling my combined accomplishment of performance art and art criticism."

The students watch Ted strut back to the trashcan. For this

occasion, a tuxedo, top hat, and wand would not have been out of place. Of course, a tight straitjacket would have been equally appropriate.

All morning, Ted has imagined this moment over and over in his mind. From his pocket, he grabs a matchbox and removes one of those nice wooden ones from it. Striking it against the box, a flame ignites for a moment but a gentle breeze snuffs it out. The students patiently watch Ted try a couple more times, with the same result. With a little trepidation, Ted moves his hands over the rim of the trashcan and strikes a match inside the can as a way to block the breeze. With a sudden whoomp, flames fly out the can. Ted hears the faint cheers of the students and jerks his head back, though not fast enough to prevent him from smelling burnt hair. The trashcan has the appropriate look of a funeral pyre. As the flames rise, Ted grabs Smead, dumps him into the can, closes the lid, and scampers for cover toward the students. The students murmur with excitement (mostly males) or put their fingers in their ears (mostly females).

Seconds go by as Ted and the students wait in anticipation. After another several seconds, nothing happens. Ted is perplexed.

"Maybe there's not enough oxygen in the can," says Rick, keenly aware of the necessary conditions for lighting up and keeping his bong going.

"Yeah, guess so. I'll do it again and this time I'll keep the lid open a bit." Ted walks toward the trashcan and just as he reaches for the lid, a deafening explosion erupts sending the lid flying into the air followed by gaseous fumes and smoke. The blast stuns Ted, and he falls back, bowled over by the explosion. As if in slow motion (audio off), the lid spins end on end in the air, reaches its apex, and then, back in real time, suddenly falls to the ground. Ted sits unsure of his condition as students rush up to both congratulate him and see if he's hurt.

"Are you OK?" asks Trudy, her hand massaging Ted's shoulder.

Ted realizes that Trudy is saying something but he cannot hear. Without sounding alarmed, he says louder than necessary, "OK, I hope you all enjoyed that, class is dismissed."

Still sitting, Ted watches his class disperse. As wisps of smoke dissipate over the can, he assesses his state and considers himself lucky that only his hearing has been affected. He suspects that his deafness (and thoroughly wet butt) will be temporary. His psychological demeanor, however, tumbles as he sees Dean Packer and Chair Franklin marching in unison toward him.

"What the hell are you doing, Ted?" yells Dean Packer.

"What?"

"Did you cause that explosion?" yells Chair Franklin.

"What?"

"What's going on?"

"What? I can't hear you. Give me a moment." Ted slowly gets up and notices that Packer and Franklin look like identical twins. Both are in suits, both are red faced, and both appear to be angry and constipated at the same time. Ted attributes this keen sense of vision to his newfound deafness.

"What the hell are you doing?" says Packer once again, now yelling right in Ted's face.

Guessing the meaning of the question, Ted responds, "I was performing an art demonstration for my class. I did use a firecracker, but it was placed in a trashcan with the lid on, and the students were at a safe distance away from it."

"That is not appropriate behavior for a faculty member. I want to see you in my office right after lunch," says the Dean.

"What? I can't really hear you right now. I think it's temporary deafness."

From his coat pocket, the Dean retrieves a pen and a pad of post-its (which he always carries for notes to his secretary). He writes, "This is serious. Come to my office at 1:30 today."

Ted reads the note and grants a sullen nod. Packer and Franklin turn their backs on Ted and head off to lunch.

Slowly, Ted collects his things. He sets his trashcan upright and notices that its sides now look like an interesting cubist sculpture or some pregnant robot torso. He peers inside the can and finds Smead nowhere in sight. Ted saunters to his car. He feels a spectrum of emotions—exhilaration, exhaustion, and sadness. At the moment, Ted is clearly experiencing post-partum depression.

6

Thursday morning—"I'm sorry I missed dinner." Ted chats causally with Clare's answering machine as he sits in his office sipping his coffee. "My call yesterday may have sounded weird because I couldn't hear what I was saying. I'm OK now, though my ears still feel like they're stuffed with cotton. I was supposed to meet with Dean Packer right after lunch, but thank goodness I could use my hearing loss as an excuse. I'll probably have to see him today. Anyway, I'll see you later at lunch, bye."

As Ted puts the phone down, he notices one of the departmental secretaries, Nancy Calder, hovering near his office door waiting for him to get off the phone. She says, "I thought you might like to see today's *Daily Nap*. You're famous, top news of the day."

Professor Sets Off Bomb on Campus!

Yesterday on the Quad, Professor Ted Shearing, from the Department of Art and Art History, provided his Introduction to Modern Art class with an "explosive" demonstration. As an example of performance art, Professor Shearing exhibited his piece that he called "Molotov Smead." He turned an art piece made by an artist named Smead into a Molotov cocktail. He poured gasoline into the glass case that housed the art work and stuffed a rag into an opening at the top. Unlike your standard Molotov cocktail, however, Professor Shearing spiked his concoction with a firecracker. He put this art work into a flaming trashcan, and to the students' delight, the thing exploded with a huge bang! Neither Professor Shearing nor any college administrators were available afterwards for comment. Students hope that Professor Shearing will continue with his art!

--Michael Gallegos, Staff Reporter

"Damn," Ted says to himself, as Nancy had graciously left him alone to read. Ted shuts his door preventing any more disruptions, but just as he does, the phone rings. Ted reluctantly picks it up, "Hullo...un-huh...yes...sure, I can be there." And now that he is scheduled to meet with the Dean after lunch, he prevents any further contact by unplugging his telephone.

"Shick, shick, shick..." On his computer, Ted watches (and can now listen to) "Rainbird in Motion." When it came in the mail yesterday, he put it on, but his deafness prevented him from hearing the soundtrack. Now, after watching for just a few minutes, he's decided that the piece is worthless, even with the soundtrack. It appears that Ted's newfound ability to express himself artistically has significantly lowered his opinion of other artists.

Ted initially planned to display Rainbird in his graduate class and have the students critique it. He was hoping to encourage the students to develop some postmodern rationalization for its existence—something like a social commentary of suburban life in the modern world. He could even suggest a sexual/masculine/power metaphor out of its nozzle or suggest that it makes a Marxist/political point. But he realizes that if Mike Gallegos can do such a decent job with an interpretation of Smead in class, what's the big deal?

Completely disheartened by Rainbird, Ted is pleased by his decision yesterday evening to go to out to Home Depot and buy a little propane blowtorch that now sits on his desk. With heightened anticipation, he plans to perform his second work of art in class today.

As students enter the room, he hears mumblings and then a voice calling out, "Hey, Professor Shearing, will you set off a bomb for our class?" That's Sid Calloway, one of the graduate students in Ted's art criticism class.

"No Sid, but I will give you a performance. I will also ask you all to write a two-page critique of my performance. It will be due on Tuesday," answers Ted.

Ted begins his lecture, "By now, you've probably all heard what I did in my Intro class yesterday. If you haven't, you can read about it in the *Daily Nap*. Basically, I expressed myself through art instead of simply teaching or criticizing it. I hope to continue with these performances for as long as my creative spirits allow. Furthermore, I hope you've all figured out that with my particular form of expression, I'm also making a not-too-subtle point about my feelings toward contemporary art."

Ted reaches into his bag and reveals a shiny DVD. He says, "I just got this in the mail yesterday. I purchased it through the internet. It's an art piece called 'Rainbird in Motion,' and if I were to show it to you, you would see a continuous video clip of one of those sprinklers, like the ones out by the Quad, doing its thing ad nauseum. I am not going to bore you with this piece. Instead, it will be part of my own work, which I call "Fire and Rainbird."

Ted pulls out the little red blowtorch from his bag. He shows it to the students and places it on the table in front of him. The students are brimming with excitement. From his bag, he pulls out a small jar of gasoline, a long screwdriver, and a disposable lighter. As in yesterday's performance, Ted allows ample time for students to peruse each fine art accessory. Finally, Ted pulls out a round aluminum pie pan, which belongs to Clare but was in Ted's cupboard after he took home some leftover apple pie. He moves to the window nearest him, pulls the cord that opens the curtains, and unlatches the window, swinging it out as wide as he can.

"Now I'm ready to perform "Fire and Rainbird." Ted feels overdressed for the occasion, so as a symbolic gesture, he rolls up his sleeves and bares his pale arms. He unscrews the cap on the jar and pours the gasoline into the pie pan. He then drops the DVD into the pan. As the Rainbird floats in the primordial pool, Ted grabs his blowtorch and turns a little screw near the nozzle. The blowtorch hisses at him in response. He holds the blowtorch in his left hand, picks up the lighter with his right, and after a couple of flicks, he succeeds in bringing the lighter's meek little flame slowly toward the hissing blowtorch. Just before he expects it to happen, a loud pop occurs and a bright flame bursts from the end of the nozzle.

Keeping the flaming blowtorch away from the pan, Ted sets the lighter down and picks up the long screwdriver. He tries to spear the DVD with the screwdriver by sticking its point into the center hole of the DVD. After a few jabs, he manages to hook it and lift the sacrificial Rainbird up over the cake pan. As it wobbles at the end of the screwdriver, dripping of gasoline, Ted slowly moves the blowtorch toward it. Again, just before he expects it to happen, flames burst and engulf the Rainbird. The flames spew black smoke as the DVD starts to melt. As Ted watches in intense fascination, he inadvertently lowers the blowtorch and manages to ignite the gasoline in the pie pan. With one hand holding the flaming Rainbird and the other holding the flaming blowtorch, Ted can do nothing about the flaming cake pan. At this moment, Ted has a flashback memory—he's sitting by a campfire with his father, holding a stick and helplessly watching flames engulf a charred marshmallow.

Except for the flaming cake pan that now appears to be losing its fuel, Ted's performance has proceeded pretty much as he imagined. Unfortunately, Ted's imagination didn't include what would happen next. As he tries to blow out the flames rising from the Rainbird, he only succeeds in increasing the amount of putrid smoke emanating from it. He moves toward the open window, wondering how many brain cells he has murdered by inhaling hydrocarbons, and continues to blow on the Rainbird. As Ted concentrates on the Rainbird, he forgets the blowtorch in his other hand, which is now pointed directly toward a now-flaming curtain. With both hands full, Ted bangs his head and shoulders against the smoldering curtain several times and snuffs outs the flames.

At this very moment across campus, someone peering out the window notices a thin trail of black smoke rising from a classroom window. Fortunately, it's Clare, who first considers that it may be Ted but then rejects the notion, thinking that he couldn't be so stupid as to perform another insane act.

The flames on the Rainbird finally peter out. Ted, winded from his huffing, puffing, and head banging, shuts off the blowtorch. For the first time since the start of his act, he realizes that he has an audience, who is now giving Ted a standing ovation. With a sheepish grin, Ted holds up his screwdriver, displaying the poor Rainbird, which hangs limply on the screwdriver, never to shick again and looking much like clockwork in a Dali painting.

At lunch, Clare admits, "You know, when I saw that smoke coming out the window I thought that it might be you, but I convinced myself that after yesterday, you wouldn't do any more stupid things." With a worried and annoyed look, she continues, "It's amazing. Today you make a DVD flambé with a blowtorch and yesterday you made a spiked Molotov cocktail. I hope you're not thinking about furthering your culinary skills."

"Well maybe I'll tone things down. But I have to tell you, I'm having fun thinking up ways of destroying my collection."

"I hope you don't destroy your career at the same time. I don't envy your meeting with the Dean. I bet he's seething after that article in the *Daily Nap*."

Ted is hit by an uneasy stomach pang, as Clare jams her fork into her spaghetti and turns it around a couple of times. He says, "Yeah, the Dean was really angry yesterday. I'm gonna get it today."

Clare continues, a little more gently, "You know you could have really hurt yourself yesterday…and today. It's sort of ironic, but in class the other day I was lecturing about a neurological case in which a guy named Phineas Gage had a freak accident in which explosives that he was setting up ignited too soon and sent an iron rod, harpoon like, through his brain. Amazingly, he didn't die, even though the rod passed clear through his frontal lobes. Phineas Gage is famous in psychology because the brain injury caused his personality to change. He went from a mild-mannered individual to an unruly guy who couldn't control his emotions. These days, there are people like Gage who show the same personality changes after banging their head, as in severe car accidents. You know, you could get a serious concussion by being so close to an explosion."

"Yeah, well, I'll be more careful," says Ted, rather nonchalantly. "You know that story reminds me of that book you gave me to read a while ago. What was it called? Something like 'The Man Who Thought His Wife was a Donut.'"

"You're thinking of "The Man Who Mistook His Wife for a Hat," answers Clare. "The collection of essays about people who had survived brain injury. Yeah, you're right, only that man had brain damage that affected his perceptions rather than his emotions. Depending on the area of the brain injured you can get different forms of mental impairment," says Clare gruffly, annoyed at Ted's nonchalance and sounding like a patronizing psychology professor. She continues, "Anyway, you can bet that the Dean won't allow you to do anymore of your performances. I wouldn't be surprised if he threatens to fire you if you try any more acts that could harm the students."

"I know, you're right...hey, I have an idea. I'll move my performances to my house. We'll have art parties. We can have one tomorrow. Maybe I can get one of Harry's cooks to help cater an outside barbeque. I'll do a performance afterwards." "How many times are you going to do this? Why don't you just get it over with at one time? You can make a big bonfire and toss your whole collection into it."

"I guess I could, but that doesn't seem very artistic."

"Oh, so now you're concerned about aesthetic destruction of your art collection?"

"I know it sounds stupid. OK, let me do this one performance tomorrow. I'll invite my students and some of the faculty, and maybe this will be the last time." With that compromise, Ted departs glumly toward the Dean's office.

Sitting in Packer's office, Ted notices the expansive view through the window and the expensive oak furniture inside. In a few moments, he hears Packer's voice. The door opens, and the twins, Packer and Franklin, walk in. Ted rises from his chair as the two enter, looking grim and carrying the aroma of a hint of white wine and garlic from some fine restaurant.

As all three sit down, Packer says, "Ted, what you did yesterday is grounds for suspension."

"I agree with the Dean, Ted. That was a crazy thing to do and as Chair I cannot condone such things," says Franklin.

Ted only nods, trying to look repentant. He realizes the twins are going to give him the bad cop-bad cop routine.

"You should know that tenure does not give you immunity from harming students and making a mockery of this campus," says Packer.

"You're not getting any support from the departmental faculty," says Franklin.

"I understand. It won't happen again," answers Ted, trying to conceal a smirk as he recalls this morning's performance.

"You're damn right, Ted," says Packer. "I've been doing damage control all morning, dealing with calls from parents and other faculty who've heard about the incident."

"Ted, I don't know what's gotten into you. Your little stunt was pure insanity and an embarrassment for the college and entire faculty," says Franklin.

"One more incident like this, Ted, and I'll initiate proceedings to have you removed from the faculty," says Packer.

"I understand," says Ted.

"You can go now," says Packer.

Ted nods, gets up, and leaves the office.

7

Friday morning—Ted unlocks his office door and pauses as he hears hammering sounds coming from down the hall. He heads toward the noise, but it stops just as he reaches Dave Connerly's office. When Ted peers into Dave's office, he sees him perched on a chair carefully hooking a frame onto the wall. The art work is hidden by Dave's head.

When Dave jumps down from his chair, revealing the piece, Ted's eyes widen. He stammers, "Where did you get that Brett Weston?"

"I got it from an internet auction. It arrived yesterday. Pretty cool, don't you think?" says Dave.

"You're slipnslide!"

"How did you know that?"

"You sniped me for that piece! I'm napart."

"Ha! Cute name. I thought you were only interested in that post-modern crap. I guess I can call it that now, since you apparently have the same opinion these days. Well maybe I saved Brett from an explosive demise."

Ted responds, "I would never destroy such a beautiful piece. I didn't know you were interested in photography."

"Well, prehistoric art is hard to come by these days. I have a small collection at home, not much."

"Speaking of explosives, I'm having a barbeque tonight at my place. I'll do a performance after dinner. It may be my last."

"Boy, you're really getting into this. Did you really set off a bomb the other day?"

"Yeah, it was fun, 'cept I nearly blew my head off. I have a few more firecrackers. Maybe I'll use some tonight. Why don't you come over?"

"Sounds like fun. I was planning on going out with my friend, Leo. She's an old grad school buddy who now lives in San Francisco. Would it be OK if she comes?"

"Sure. Leo, that's an odd name for a woman."

"Her real name is Leona. Actually, she might be interested in your performance. Leo turned her back on academia to become an art critic for the *Chronicle*. Hey, maybe you'll get a write-up!"

"I don't know if that would be good or bad. I had this meeting with Packer and Franklin yesterday and boy, were they pissed. They threatened to fire me if I conducted any more performances on campus."

"I guess setting off bombs on campus isn't what professors are supposed to do. But hey, you're from Berkeley!" says Dave, thinking that seniority in the department may come sooner for him than anticipated.

"Yeah, right. Anyway, come on over around six tonight. Bring Leo and feel free to let anyone else in the department know about it. I'm also going to invite the students from my class."

Ted strolls down the hall to the classroom. He writes on the chalkboard, "Professor Shearing's class is cancelled today. Instead, you are all invited to dinner and a performance tonight at my place—6 pm, 26 Hilltop Lane."

Back in his office, Ted sends a general email invitation to all departmental faculty and students. He calls Clare and leaves a message that he won't be around for lunch as he needs to prepare for tonight's party. With academic duties relieved for the day, Ted heads home to plan his party and performance.

After a side trip to the market and few phone calls, Ted has dinner in place. For a price, Harry Burns will send over one of his cooks, who will prepare BBQ chicken and sausages. He also enlisted "The Veggie Van," a local catering service, to provide vegetarian entrees and desserts. At the market, Ted got drinks, paper plates, and plasticware.

His phone rings. "Hullo."

"Hi," says Clare, "Just wanted to see if you needed any help for the party."

"Nope. I've got everything planned. A cook from 'The Elegant Cave' will man the barbeque, and I got 'The Veggie Van' to provide the rest."

"That's great. You're not going to put us all in danger tonight with one of your antics are you?" asks Clare, apprehensively.

"I was just about to sit down and think about what I'm gonna do. I'm figuring that this will be my last performance..." Ted's sentence trails off as he thinks to himself, "...and I want to go out with a bang."

"Well, we'll come over around 6. I should say, your stature with Kevin has risen significantly."

"Great. Come a little early if you can and Kevin can help me set up, and feel free to invite anyone from the Psych Department. There'll be plenty of food."

"OK. I'll do that. See you then. Bye." Clare makes a mental note not to invite clinical faculty who might diagnose her mate as a total nut case.

Ted sits on his sofa and opens his mind to any creative spirits that may wish to enter. His palette of firecrackers, gasoline, and blowtorch sit in a box next to him. Reasonable judgment (and Clare) tells him to avoid a potentially dangerous performance. On the other hand, four Red Devils peer out from the box eagerly waiting for some action.

Ted's conception begins to form. He grabs a roll of duct tape and scissors from his desk, then snips off some tape and places it temporarily onto his pinky. Returning to the sofa, he reaches into the box and grabs the four Red Devils. He aligns them so that all of the fuses are at the same end. He wraps the tape around the Red Devils, making a snug little bundle. With scissors, he snips the fuses off of three of the four firecrackers. He then ties the fuses together, end to end, thus making one long knotted fuse coming out of the bundle of firecrackers.

Satisfied with his explosive device, Ted considers his art collection. He walks over to the closet in his spare bedroom and slides open the door, revealing dozens of large cardboard boxes filled with his collection. In front of the boxes are two bright orange sawhorse-shaped stands, the kind used around construction sites and road work. Strung between the two stands is official-looking police tape on which is printed, "Off Limits. Do Not Cross," which happens to be the name of the art piece. Ted first saw the piece displayed against a wall in the San Diego Museum of Art as part of an exhibition of emerging West Coast artists. The artist, Diane Noxzema, pilfered the stands from a road construction site in downtown LA. Ted is not quite sure why he bought "Off Limits. Do Not Cross," but it's now quite valuable. Diane's other pieces, "Closed for Repairs" and "Warning. Slippery When Wet," have also been exhibited and are exactly the same as "Off Limits..." except for what is printed on the yellow tape. Needless to say, Diane's work has been largely ignored by the general public, except "Closed for Repairs," which elicited numerous complaints by museumgoers as Diane demanded the piece be exhibited in front of the men's restroom. Yet to art critics and revelers of modernity, Noxzema's feminist statements are considered stunning and incisive works.

Ted grabs the two stands, bundles the yellow strands of plastic tape, and drags the art work into the living room. He sets the stands facing each other, figuring he can use them as support onto which the main performance piece can rest. With a sly grin, Ted swings around, reaches over his sofa, and removes from its hook his most valuable piece, "Lost Souls #4." He sets the piece onto the two stands. He then picks up the bundle of Red Devils and places it snugly into a fluffy pink slipper that's glued near in the center of the canvas. The fuse dangles out from the slipper like a ratty shoelace.

It's six-thirty and Clare and Kevin are the only guests who have arrived so far. The caterer from "The Veggie Van" busily sets serving bowls onto tables. Hans Bergerac, from "The Elegant Cave," slow-cooks chicken and sausages on an industrial-sized gas grill. Kevin sits in the living room next to Ted's performance piece, playing a game on his cell phone. Clare and Ted hastily distribute cups, utensils, and paper plates onto tables.

Muffled car sounds from down the hill signal a caravan of

cars snaking its way up. The cars park next to Ted's house, and shortly after loads of students pile out. One of them yells, "Hi, Professor Shearing."

Ted waves and answers, "Hi, Gang. Make yourself comfortable. Grab a drink, dinner will be ready shortly."

Some of the students head for the ice chest filled with beer, while others spread out and fling a Frisbee. Ted's pleased that the students have come to see his performance. The students are pleased to get free dinner.

Heading back to the house, Ted sees Kevin in the living room and says, "Hey, I have to thank you for initiating, or shall I say 'sparking' my art interest."

"Gee, Ted, it's pretty outrageous. I guess I have to thank you for getting mom off my back. She stopped hassling me about Santa Rosa after you started your thing. Mom is totally pissed at you."

Ted never thought he would be bonding with Kevin in this way—as partners in vandalism. Trying to keep up a modicum of adult behavior, Ted says, "Well, I told your mom that this will be my last performance."

"Kinda cool that you taped those firecrackers together like that."

"Yeah, well, after my first performance, I had these four left over, and as this will be my last, I thought I'd just get rid of them all at once. Check out my makeshift fuse. I tied all four fuses together to make a longer one. That will allow me more time to clear out after I light it."

"Cool. Yeah, mom said you nearly killed yourself with one firecracker."

"Well. Uh, that's an exaggeration, but still, I was pretty stupid getting too close to that first one. Anyway, it'll be fun watching this one go off. After dinner, will you help me carry this thing out?"

"Sure. I'll even help you light it, if you like."

"Well, if I let you do that, your mom will castrate me." Ted feels amazingly comfortable with Kevin. Perhaps he can guide Kevin's interests, "But you know, the San Francisco Museum of Modern Art has lots of cool and sort of twisted exhibits. Why don't we all go out there some time?"

"Sure. This girl I know, Jenny, she's into art and stuff. Maybe I can ask her to come along with us."

"Sure. Why don't we go out now and see if dinner's ready?"

Ted and Kevin walk out the back door and are met with the smoky aroma of grilled meat. Clare sees them and excuses herself from the small group of psychology faculty.

"Hey, you two," says Clare. "Looks like we're ready to eat. All the plates are out."

"Great. I'll go around and tell everyone. Kevin, will you go down the hill and tell the students that they can come up for some grub?"

"Sure."

"Great food." says Dave Connerly, a sausage dangling at the end of his fork. "Oh yeah. Let me introduce you to Leona."

Ted turns toward Leona and is quickly mesmerized by a stunningly beautiful woman with flows of dark Mediterranean hair, a shapely figure, and sensuous smile. With minimal make-up and simply dressed, Leona radiates the kind of natural beauty that makes most men conjure prurient thoughts or spontaneous marriage proposals. She says, "Hi. Most people call me Leo."

"Hullo," stutters Ted, almost speechless, having just undressed her mentally and still reeling from the thought.

"Hey Ted," says Dave. "What's on the menu for performance art tonight?"

Leo adds, "Yes, Dave told me about your foray into art expression. It certainly sounds interesting."

Chomping on his sausage, Dave warns, "You better watch out what you say, Ted. You might regret what appears in the paper tomorrow."

"Well it should be fun," says Ted, and turning to Leo, "so you're an art critic for the *Chronicle*?"

"Yes. I decided that the academic route was too much hassle and anyway who needs another Italian Renaissance scholar. I guess I'm more the here and now type. But I suppose there's a lot of rationalizing there, as I do envy the professorial life sometimes. Anyway, I've learned a lot since working for the *Chron*, and I do get to travel a bit."

"Sounds like an interesting job," says Ted.

"Yeah, Leo's getting more and more column space all the time. I'm counting on her being on TV soon," says Dave.

"No, that's not for me. Too showy. I hate all that glitzy stuff. I like the writing. I can present my views and probably be read by more people than if I had ended up in academia."

"That's for sure," says Dave.

"I agree, even tenure isn't all that it's cracked up to be," says Ted, trying hard not to stare at Leo and curious about the depth of Dave's relationship with her.

Just then Clare strolls over and slips her arm around Ted's. "Hi," she says to the group.

"Hi Clare," says Dave, "this is my friend Leo."

"Hi, nice to meet you," says Clare, extending her hand.

"Hi," says Leo, smiling and shaking Clare's hand.

"Clare's my partner. She's on the psychology faculty at Napa State," says Ted trying hard to suppress the more primitive parts of his brain.

"Hey Clare," says Dave, "What would a psychologist say about Ted's newfound creative outlet?"

"No comment," says Clare.

Ted blushes, but Dave and Leo both laugh.

Breaking the awkward moment, Leo says, "Well, the art world could certainly use something new and really innovative. Most of what's out there is rather vapid."

"I agree," says Ted, still having difficulty carrying a conversation with Leo, especially with Clare at his side. He excuses himself and mingles with others. Drifting about, he sees Ed Sparta advancing toward him. Ed, a handsome, stocky fellow, is a metalwork artist in the department.

Ed says, "Hey Ted, I noticed that charred and bloated trashcan by your house."

"Yeah," says Ted, "That was from my first performance. What do you think?"

"Interesting. I might be able to do something with it. Perhaps weld some of my forms to the side. It could be our collaboration."

"Sounds like fun, but I'm keeping the stuff I use in my performances as mementos. I'm also keeping a record of them by photographing before and after images. But you know, I can tell you how to make your own. All it takes is some gasoline and a firecracker."

"Sure, maybe, but it sounds a little hazardous," says Ed. "I do like the way it looks."

It's dessert time, and Ted excuses himself to prepare for his performance. He heads to the living room and finds Kevin on the sofa watching TV.

"Hey Kevin. It's almost show time. Will you help me get this thing outside?"

"Sure," says Kevin, hitting the remote and turning off the TV.

"Great. I'll lift this and you take the stands. Be careful to grab all that yellow tape." With accessories in hand, Kevin and Ted walk out to the yard, past the tables, and near the crest of the hill. Students are gathered nearby, chatting in the afterglow of sunset. Ted's pleased that most of the students are still around for his performance.

"OK Kevin, can you set the stands here just like they were in the living room?"

"Sure," says Kevin.

The guests, having noticed Ted and Kevin making preparations, saunter over. Ted sets "Lost Souls #4" on the stands and says to Kevin, "OK, I'm putting you in charge of security. I'm going back to the house to get a few more things."

"Sure thing."

Ted walks briskly to the house. The excitement of performing sends butterflies aflutter in his stomach. He passes Clare on his way. She has an odd expression—the top half of her face is frowning, but the bottom half is weakly smiling. Ted says, "I promise I'll be careful."

"OK, I love you," says Clare.

"Love you, too."

In the living room, Ted reaches into his box and retrieves the gasoline can and lighter. The thought of Leona watching his performance adds to the excitement. He trots out the house, looking like a prize fighter entering the ring.

The guests gather around, but they also give Ted a wide berth, not completely trusting his pyrotechnical skills. They are perfectly segregated—faculty on one side, students on the other. For all, there's a feeling of Fourth of July in the air.

Ted looks for Clare and sees her in the very back behind Kevin. Her arms are wound tightly around Kevin's waist, as if to guarantee that he's kept at a safe distance. Dave and Leo are in the front chatting, smiling, and looking rather fondly at each other.

Ted yells, "OK, thanks for staying for my performance. Tonight is really special. I have here two works of contemporary art from my collection. One is called "Off Limits. Do Not Cross" and the other is called "Lost Souls #4." Both students and faculty snicker at the titles. Leo turns to Dave and nods approvingly at the selection. Ted continues, "These two pieces will be part of my performance, which I call 'Immaterial Soles.'"

Ted lifts "Lost Souls #4" off the stands and places it on the grass. He unscrews the cap from the gasoline can, tips the can, and attempts to dribble a little gas onto "Off Limits..." Instead, he inadvertently douses the two stands, splashing the gas around the ground and on his shirt. He puts "Lost Souls #4" back onto the stands and pours gasoline all over the canvas, making sure that each shoe, slipper and boot gets its share. He recaps the gasoline can and places it on the grass away at a safe distance.

Turning to the crowd, Ted yells, "OK, I'm ready. So here goes 'Immaterial Soles.'"

Ted sticks his hand into his pocket and retrieves the lighter. He flicks it and holds down the little lever, so he can display the little flame to his audience. The students "ooh" and "ahh" in mock anticipation. The faculty is silent, yet curious. Kevin is wide-eyed; Clare is tight-lipped. Dave and Leo are still smiling at each other.

Slowly, Ted bends over. He can smell the fumes emanating

from the footwear. He brings the lighter close to the long, knotted fuse. When the little flame kisses the fuse, a bright glow erupts. Ted runs quickly back to the crowd, his head down, as if in a scene of a bad action movie. Turning back to the piece, he watches the end of the fuse shorten, making little bright flashes each time the sizzling fuse comes to a knot.

As the last of the stringed fuses shortens and disappears into the darkness of the pink slipper, a brilliant flash illuminates the area. The flash is followed by a resounding explosion that reverberates through the crowd and down the hill. At the same moment, bright flames engulf the canvas and stands, sending sparks and smoke up into the night sky. The students cheer boisterously; while on the faculty side, Ted is greeted by smiles and appreciative applause. Clare, thoroughly relieved that no one is hurt, hangs more loosely onto Kevin who is cheering in sheer delight. Ted solemnly bows to his audience.

8

In the Arts Section of the Sunday *San Francisco Chronicle*, Ted reads:

Performance Art Explodes!

by Leona D'Angelo

Just when you thought that performance art was dead, a new artist appears on the scene. In our own nearby hamlet of Napa, Ted Shearing, Professor of Art History at the State College, performs what I can only describe as artistic anarchy. In his fiendishly provocative performances, Ted Shearing breaks all the rules; he destroys art.

On Friday, I witnessed a performance. Previously, Shearing's work had only been seen by students in his class. On this warm spring night, he entertained dinner guests by dousing with gasoline two highly regarded works of contemporary art—Anita Fleming's "Lost Souls #4" and Diane Noxzema's "Off Limits. Do Not Disturb." He then placed firecrackers in the middle of these two pieces and proceeded to annihilate them in a performance he entitled, "Immaterial Souls" (or perhaps "Immaterial Soles").

State of the Arts

What is this man doing? It seems that Professor Shearing, in his bold, and dare I say, explosive approach, is throwing out the window all that is near and dear to contemporary art. In one artfully destructive move, he literally ruined its foundation, shunning social realism, feminism, aesthetics, morality, and sanity.

I spoke with the artist after his performance. This seemingly mild-mannered professor is fed up with contemporary art and isn't going to take it anymore. Over the years, he has collected over 100 works by upstart artists, some of whom, like Fleming and Noxzema, have risen to the top of the contemporary art world. Yet recently, Professor Shearing has taken the side of what can be considered the general public's view of contemporary art—that art these days is nothing more than inane trash, worthy of creative annihilation.

Never mind the five-figure prices of these works. Ted considers most of what is exhibited these days as trite, jam-it-in-your-face metaphors or symbolic conceptualizations which probably would have been best left as concepts. I must agree. The thing is, denigration of what's new and hip in art is the kiss of death for critics (maybe this one!) and other shareholders of the commodity we call art. How far will Professor Shearing go? It appears that the artist has his limits. He wouldn't think of destroying most hallmark works of modern art. Indeed, he says he wouldn't even consider destroying what is exhibited in SF MOMA, even if he could afford the pieces. Thus, Diebenkorn, Hesse, Thiebaud, and others—both dead and alive—can rest in peace.

Yet what about all of those upstart artists living in meager existences in barely affordable lofts or shabby studios in art centers like New York, London, or San Francisco? Beware! Ted Shearing is on the loose and ready to include your work in his next performance. At least you might become famous in one brief flash of recognition. In any event, Ted Shearing, the Anarchist of Art, is sure to be vehemently hated and jealously loved by the art world.

Ted closes his eyes, takes a deep breath, and puts down the paper. Within a minute, the phone rings. In fact, for the rest of the day, the phone rings and rings. In the afternoon, TV crewmen and recognizable news anchors trek up the hill to seek interviews. Ted, the artist, has arrived.

9

"These days art can be anything," asserts Ted to Clare, Kevin, and Jenny as they drive toward San Francisco. Jenny, Kevin's new girl friend (but not a 'girlfriend' according to Kevin), loves philosophy and enjoys engaging others in intellectual banter.

"So, I can proclaim that this car and us in it is a work of art?" asks Jenny.

"Sure, some say that it's merely the intention of the artist that deems something a work of art. You may know, Duchamp took a men's urinal, set it on its back, and christened it art. One fellow even called a real horse a 'Work of Art' as it was a champion racehorse."

Ted finds the conversation refreshing and usefully distracting as it settles his nerves. This afternoon at SF CONART, Ted will give his first public performance. Leona's article stirred curiosity within the art world. She called this morning to tell him that a prominent New York critic will be attending.

"But that means there's no sense in deciding if something is art or not. What's the point if anything can be called 'art'?"

demands Kevin excitedly, not wanting to be left behind and eager to impress Jenny. Together in the back seat, Kevin can't help but sense Jenny's warmth and subtle fragrance. Jenny turns to Kevin and smiles, as if he's just scored from three-point range.

"Yup," smiles Ted, glancing in the rear-view mirror and pleased by the growing closeness between the two in the back. He turns to Clare, who knows without even looking what's evolving in the back seat.

As Ted follows the cars onto the Golden Gate Bridge, he notices the girders glistening in the unusually bright morning. Tiny sailboats dot the bay, tilted by strong winds, though on the bridge the breeze blows cool and relaxed.

"So, how does one define art?" asks Jenny.

"Good question!" says Ted. "It's not clear and some have serious concerns about the state of art today. I'm beginning to feel that contemporary art has wallowed too much in what might be called "meta-art" or art as intellectual commentary about art. Over the years, the definition of art has broadened to include anything, but particularly cute puns and silly references about what an art object is. When I look at most contemporary art today, I cringe at how much idiocy exists out there. Recently, I've become completely disheartened by it. You'll see when we get to the museum. I warn you guys, most of the stuff in there is really stupid. It's much more fun to go to a photography gallery than look at the stuff at CONART. In some ways, art has lost the pleasures of life, of being."

"That's interesting." Clare remarks. "One could think of art as having lost its body, of having lost the idea that viewing art is a human experience. In cognitive science, there's an interesting proposal that argues that the way we communicate—our language—is not based on an abstract set of rules, symbols or concepts. Our language and indeed our thoughts are tied closely to our bodies. For instance, we often think in terms of bodily feelings as metaphors, such as something is 'too hot to handle' or someone is 'near' to us. In other words, our thoughts are inextricably linked to our bodies. A prominent professor at Cal says we have 'embodied minds'."

"Very interesting. We need an embodied art, one in which the sense of feeling and seeing is given as much importance as the conceptual issues. Contemporary art has lost its body. Clare, we should think about this some more—we can call it an 'embodied aesthetics.'"

The two in the back lose interest in embodied aesthetics and instead gain interest in each other's bodies.

"How 'bout we hit Bill's Burgers for lunch?" suggests Clare.

"Great for me," Ted agrees, as the two in the back nod approvingly.

As the waitress sets down a monstrous burger in front of Jenny, she asks: "But if art can be anything, how does one determine if an artwork is good or bad?"

"Yes, that's the issue now." says Ted. "Some think that the way we evaluate art needs revision. Of course, my own view is that quite a lot of contemporary art is junk."

"But do you think all abstract art is bad?" asks Jenny.

"No." answers Ted, his voice muffled by a mouthful of a "Dean Martin" burger, famous for its melted Provolone and splash of marinara sauce. After swallowing, he continues, "For much of the 20th century, abstract art made wonderful and incredibly interesting statements about what art can be. Artists didn't have to paint objects of things. Instead, they could play with the medium, express themselves, explore the notion of what paint can do."

"So how do you tell good abstract art from bad stuff?" asks Kevin.

"Well, for one thing, it's important to think about what an artist is trying to say about the act of painting. Some very novel works were accomplished by trying to break away from the natural three-dimensionality of space, while others tried to minimize painting to its very essence, such as lines, basic geometric forms and colors. Some artists extended borders, such as breaking the barrier between painting and sculpture. We need to go to SF MOMA sometime."

"I never thought of abstract art like that," says Jenny. "I've always preferred the Impressionists. When you put it that way it means you really have to know the background or ideas behind an artwork to appreciate it. You need to understand it."

"That's right! To appreciate much of modern art, it is very important to understand the conceptual or intellectual history of its evolution. I think that really good art, be it abstract or otherwise, needs more…it needs to be visually interesting, it needs to hit you emotionally. The problem for me is that after the 60s, much of what was shown as new art started to lose its visual and emotional aesthetics."

"You know," says Clare, "once again, we can bring in psychology. In my Psych 1 course, I identify three basic aspects of our minds—perceiving, thinking, and feeling. The way you put it, post-modern art is over-indulgent of the thinking part and has lost the perceiving and feeling parts."

"Exactly! Great way of putting it. We need to get to a more balanced art, one that is more in line with our psyche—an embodied aesthetic." In excitement, Ted stuffs the rest of the burger in his mouth.

"That's cool." says Kevin, "But what does that say about YOUR art performance at CONART?"

"Ouch. I guess my 'art,' if you want to call it that, is making its own statement about the kind of stuff that I'm destroying. With respect to visual and emotional impact, I guess you'd have to say it's pretty cool playing with a blowtorch and putting things on fire."

"Can't argue with that!" says Kevin, giving Ted a high-five across the table.

On the drive to SF CONART, Ted feels contentedly balanced. He is buoyed by the stimulating conversation, yet weighted by the Dean Martin burger. Indeed, everyone in the car is content just to peer out the window and reflect upon sights, thoughts, and intestinal feelings. As they cross the city and head toward Market Street, Ted notices Jenny and Kevin, though silent, sit a tad closer to each other than before.

In this peaceful moment, Ted considers today's upcoming performance. He has chosen a truly inane piece to annihilate—*Play-Doh's Republic*. The artwork now sits in the trunk next to a blowtorch. The piece, sculpted by Hector Shapiro, consists of a colorfully molded structure made with the popular child's clay. At its base is what looks to be an oversized replica of the volume of Plato's work that Hector used in a college philosophy course. The volume opens to a page in the middle and on top of it rests a three-dimensional rendition of what looks like Raphael's *School of Athens*—a molded hall with an arched ceiling, and two little clay figures standing in the middle, presumably Plato and Aristotle. Along the edges of the hall are crudely molded figures in various postures.

Ted selected *Play-Doh's Republic* for his performance today because the piece was originally displayed at SF CONART in an exhibition of up and coming artists (though after the exhibit Shapiro went down and out). Ted found the piece at Hugh Gray's gallery a few months later and bought it for teaching purposes, as a way of introducing Plato's view on art, imitation, and aesthetics. It usually gets a good chuckle from students. Recently, however, Ted simply shows a slide of the art work and thus can dispense with the actual sculpture, which he detests. In his class, Ted argues that the piece represents a socio-political commentary, signifying the juxtaposition of a classical utopian society with its medium, *Play-Doh*, which represents the frivolity, fragility, and commercial application of a child's clay toy. At this moment, however, the critical epistemological issue is to what extent *Play-Doh* is flammable.

"Hey, we're at the museum," Ted remarks as he drives into a private lot at the back of SF CONART. Ted switches the engine off and turns to the others, "Leona said she'd meet us at the back door."

The group climbs out of the car. When Ted reaches the Museum door, he pushes an intercom button and waits.

"Yes, who is it?" a tinny speaker voice says.

"Hello, it's Ted Shearing and company. Leona D'Angelo told me to meet her here."

"Yes, of course. She'll be down in a moment."

In a moment, Ted sees Leona through the glass door coming down the hall with Dave Connerly and another woman.

As the door opens, a perky young woman says, "Hello, I'm Sarah Steadman, I'm the Assistant Director. Please to meet you Professor Shearing."

"Hi. Call me Ted. This is Clare, Kevin, and Jenny."

"Hello all," says Sarah.

"Hello Ted," says Leona warmly, as she steps up and gives him a hug.

Ted exercises mindful suppression, trying hard not to think about Leona's firm breasts pressing against him, tantamount to not thinking about pink elephants or actually pink flesh.

In turn, Leona hugs Clare and shakes hands with Kevin and Jenny. Dave steps up and says, "Well Professor Shearing, interesting extracurricular activities! Looks like you've made it big time."

"Thanks Dave," says Ted, though in his mind Ted thinks that a performance at SF CONART is hardly 'big time.'

"Come this way." says Sarah.

"Oh, could you wait a minute," says Ted, "I need to get my stuff out of the car. Hey Kevin, Dave, could you help me?"

"Sure," Kevin and Dave say in unison.

As the others stand and chat, Ted, Kevin, and Dave head for the car and return with *Play-Doh's Republic*, blowtorch, aluminum tray, and can of gasoline.

"OK, I'm ready...oh, wait." Ted sets *Play-Doh's Republic* on the ground, unzips his shoulder bag and rummages through it until he fondles a book of matches. "OK, I'm ready now."

The group, led by Sarah, meanders left and right through hallways that ultimately lead to a double door. She escorts everyone through the doors, which puts them in a dark room until Sarah flicks on a light switch. The group finds themselves in a small dressing room, which looks like an odd combination of locker room and cheap motel. Against one wall are metal cabinets, a long bench, and mirror, and against the other is an old sofa and side table.

Sarah moves across the room, props open another door at the opposite end and says, "Ted, you'll find our little theater through this door past the curtains."

"Great," says Ted, holding *Play-Doh's Republic* and motioning Dave and Kevin to follow him through the door

When Ted enters the theatre, he finds it looks more like an elementary school classroom. The walls appear to be adorned with this semester's art projects, which actually are works by contemporary artists, though many visitors have remarked, "My kid could paint that." A large table sits at front of the room with several rows of folding metal chairs placed behind it.

The only peculiar, though clearly appropriate, addition to the room is a tall Plexiglas barrier that stands between the table and front row of chairs. Ted chuckles, imagining himself as the Pope in public, protected from crazy terrorists by the bulletproof shield. Of course, in this situation it is the audience that needs protection.

Dave bobs his head toward the barrier and remarks, "I guess Sarah was worried that you might kill us all."

"Well, I'm only gonna set this thing on fire...but I imagine for insurance purposes, the museum has got to protect their clientele as best they can."

Ted continues, "Kevin, could you put the tray on the table. Dave, just set the blowtorch and can on the floor."

Ted places *Play-Doh's Republic* inside the aluminum tray and says to Kevin and Dave, "Great. Thanks. I'll spend a few minutes getting prepared. We have about an hour before show time. Why don't you guys look around the museum, and when I'm done, I'll come looking for you all."

"Sure thing, Maestro," answers Dave.

Alone now, Ted feels the jitters of his first public

performance. He reaches down, grabs the blowtorch and can of gasoline, and places them on the table. He retrieves the matchbox from his bag and sets it next to the blowtorch. He also retrieves a small camera from his bag, moves around the Plexiglas barrier, and sits on the front row, center chair. He flicks the camera on and raises it up to frame his setup. With a click, he documents his first public performance.

Satisfied, Ted exits the room and enters the public halls of SF CONART. He looks around and sees a few visitors admiring the exhibits. He then looks at the wall in front of him and sees a piece which confirms Ted's sentiment about contemporary art. A huge flat-paneled LCD screen flashes in bright red letters, "Beat Me...Beat Me..." This message alternates with flashes of "Meat Be...Meat Be..."

Strolling down the hall, Ted looks into several gallery rooms until he finds Clare, Kevin, Jenny, Leona, and Dave grouped around a gumball machine placed in the middle of a room. Huge piles of pennies have been placed on the floor around the machine. Ted approaches and watches Kevin stoop down, pick up a penny, and stick it into the machine.

"Hiya," says Ted.

As the group turns their attention to Ted, Kevin points to the gumball machine and says, "Hey Ted, check this out! What do you make of it?"

Ted, maneuvering around piles of pennies on the floor, notices the glass globe in which the multicolored gumballs sit, ready to be dispensed. On the glass, in flowery cursive writing, is printed, "Capitalist Chews."

"Cute," says Ted, "What color did you get?"

"A green one," says Kevin, as he pops it into his mouth.

"Remember what I said in the car about this museum?" admonishes Ted to Kevin.

"Yup, but hey, there's some wild stuff here, and free gumballs!" says Kevin, as he stoops down to retrieve another penny.

"Wait." says Clare, "One's enough."

"OK." says Kevin, giving the penny to Jenny, who smiles back.

"At this time, I'd like to bring out Ted Shearing!" announces Leona to the polite audience.

Entering from behind the curtain, Ted sees Leona standing next to the table clapping with the audience. Clare, Kevin, Jenny, Dave, and an unknown bearded fellow comprise the front row; behind them are about twenty well-dressed visitors.

Ted begins, "Thank you. As Leona mentioned, this is my first public appearance. It's truly an honor to present my art here at CONART." Ted pauses momentarily after that last sentence, remembering his warning to Kevin.

He continues, "My own interests have moved me from merely teaching about art to developing my own way of artistic expression. You see, it seems that art has lost its soul, its life." Ted would like to spend the next half hour lecturing about the stupidity of contemporary art, but he notices vacant stares and restless squeaking of chairs. He ends quickly, "so, anyway, let me get started..."

Ted uncaps the gasoline can and begins to pour some into the aluminum tray and onto *Play-Doh's Republic*. After drenching the piece, he screws the cap back onto the can and puts it down behind him.

As gas fumes begin to permeate the area, Ted says "Today's performance is called 'Plato's Inferno With Feats of Clay'."

As the crowd watches, Ted picks up the box of matches, strikes a match, and guardedly tosses the match into the tray. With an air-sucking whoomp, flames engulf *Playdoh's Republic*, and for a moment, the piece looks like Atlanta in "Gone With the Wind." The sculptured walls flare, charring from the bottom up, with yellow-blue flames blazing out of clay windows. The flaming arched ceiling crumbles onto poor Plato and Aristotle, as the entire piece melts away in a glorious immolation scene.

As the flames die out, the audience applauds politely. Kevin expresses the most enthusiasm, clapping vigorously in rhythm to his gumball chewing. Sarah moves quickly to open both the front and rear doors, as the room now smells like a live TV cooking show gone terribly awry.

The audience filters out, having been amused by the show, yet wondering exactly what the point was. Many are particularly relieved that their children didn't see this, as they are thinking, "My kid could do that."

"Very nice, Ted," says Leona, the first to greet Ted.

Next to Leona stands the bearded fellow who sat in the front row. Extending his hand, he says, "Hello, my name is Felix Markman. Very interesting. I work for *Art Review*."

"Yes." says Leona, "Felix flew in from New York to see the Manet exhibit at the Legion of Honor, but he also wanted to see your performance. Felix would like to interview you for *Art Review*. Would you mind spending a few minutes with him? Sarah says we can use the back room."

"Sure. I think so," says Ted as he looks up to see Clare, Kevin, Jenny, and Dave surrounding him.

Clare pipes up, "No problem. Take your time. We'll hang out and meet you at the gift store when you're done."

"OK," says Ted.

Leona leads Ted and Felix to the back and says, "Thanks again, Ted, that was really nice. I'll leave you and Felix alone."

"Thanks," says Ted as he and Felix sit down on the sofa.

"Well, Ted, I find your art and commentary very provocative. The destruction of art as art is curiously titillating. Can you fill me in on your stance?"

"You know, art has lost the pleasures of life, of being..."

10

"Please turn off all electronic devices and make sure your tray table is in the full upright and locked position. We will be arriving at Los Angeles International Airport in just a few minutes." Ted closes his novel and prepares for landing. During the months since his performance at SF CONART and as a result of Felix Markman's review, Ted's status in the art world has skyrocketed. Embraced by many critics, Ted's art has risen to the top of the heap, as it were; and the moniker, "Anarchist of Art," has stuck. Ted was prominently featured in *Artforum* and now receives thousands of emails daily, including performance invitations, artists volunteering their work to be used by Ted, and marriage proposals—with attached photos of individuals, both male and female, often skimpily clad in black leather. Ted enjoys the correspondences, though he does receive the occasional death threats. Last month, Ted was Clare's hero by having been interviewed on *The Colbert Report*, her favorite TV show.

Recognition at Napa State has been less welcoming. When Dean Packard heard about the "Fire and Rainbird" performance, he used the charred curtain as evidence of Ted's unstable behavior. Ted was immediately put on suspended leave without pay and awaits a hearing later this month by a committee that will review the future status of his employment. No one at the college has stepped up in support of Ted's actions. Indeed, despite enormous fame in the art world, Ted will likely be terminated from his academic position by the end of the year.

The "Fasten Your Seatbelt" sign blinks off, and Ted rises slowly from his seat. He reaches up, unlatches the overhead bin, and retrieves his suitcase. As he juggles it down from its perch, Ted feels the fatigue of a two-week traveling art show. On this trip, he has visited museums in Cleveland, Denver, and Houston, and will now hit LA before returning home. A sharp, almost physical, pain hits him as he contemplates today's schedule, a routine that he has repeated at each museum visit: pick-up by some perky host, lunch with benefactors, preparation for his show, and fun with blowtorch and gasoline.

Ted shuffles down the aisle, eyes fixated on the patterned carpet in front of him. Sighing, he moves glumly out of the airplane and onto the gangplank. As he enters the airport terminal, he looks up expecting to see a perky host holding a placard with his name on it. Instead, he is confronted by waves of boisterous screams. An erratic crowd jams the gateway seemingly to get a glimpse of a perpetrator. Ted stops suddenly as cameras flash and television crews push their way toward him. Loud mutterings, which sound like "There he is!" are heard. The crowd's expression and pointing fingers suggest something tragic has happened, and Ted is to blame. Ted looks behind, desperately hoping that the focus is on someone else. He considers slinking back into the tight womb of the Boeing 767, but abandons all hope when a finely dressed man with a CNN patch on his sports coat bumps against Ted and shoves a microphone in his face.

"I suppose you're unaware of what happened just a little over an hour ago?" asks the handsome and vaguely familiar looking newsman.

"What's going on?"

"Apparently, someone tried to ram a car into the entrance of the Los Angeles Modern Art Museum."

"What!"

"Yes, a guy drove his car up onto the pedestrian walkway and headed toward the museum. He drove at a fairly fast clip and almost hit some folks on the way. His intent was to drive into the museum and ruin as much art as he could. Fortunately, he couldn't get past the statue in front of the museum and simply rammed into it. The statue, I believe by Rodin, is fine, the guy isn't seriously injured, but his Toyota is totaled. The police arrived and found the guy rocking back and forth in his car with a crazed look and muttering, 'Damn Rodin, damn Balzac, I'm better than Shearing!' What do you make of it?"

"My God, that's insane," says Ted, not the most loquacious of interviewees.

As the crowd pushes closer, the interviewer asks, "Given your performances in which you've destroyed the works of various contemporary artists and given your namesake as the 'Anarchist of Art' I wonder if you could tell us what you think of individuals who go around doing such things. Clearly this is a case of a copycat artist."

Sweat builds on Ted's forehead. He sputters, "Well, of course I think it's crazy. I would never try to hurt anyone, and I certainly don't condone damaging museums. One could consider this one of the dangers of art." Ted surprises himself by this last remark. After blurting it out, he wasn't actually sure what he meant by it. Was it about himself, about museums, or figuratively about the state of the art?

Before the newsman pops another question, a large, well-built fellow intervenes between Ted and the newsman. "Hello, I'm Neil Sternum, Chief Director of the Los Angeles Modern Art Museum. I will be escorting Professor Shearing to the museum. He is a guest of our institution, and any further questions can be directed to our PR department."

With help from airport security, Ted and Neil make their way through the airport and out to a limousine.

Inside the dark comfort of the limo, Ted calms down, turns to Neil, and says, "Thanks for saving me from that crowd."

"Well, it's been a hectic morning. Frankly, we were so concerned that we almost decided to cancel your performance. But I consulted our staff, and most of us agree that artists can't control who they influence and thus can't be responsible for the actions of others. If we were to cancel your performance, it would have infringed on those of us, including me, who value the freedom of artistic expression."

"I'm dumbfounded by the actions of this psychotic, and I certainly appreciate the way you're handling the situation."

"When we get back to LAMA, you'll meet Sally, our Director of Contemporary Art, who was originally going to pick you up. You can hang out in her office until lunch. Rather than dining at a local restaurant as we had planned, Sally will have food catered into the museum. I've already asked her to contact the guests about the change in plans. I won't be able to join you as I've scheduled a press conference at noon. I'll dismiss this morning's event as a singular act by an insane individual. I will also mention that your performance will go on this afternoon as scheduled. Be prepared to have a full house. We've already been called by TV stations for permission to set up their video equipment."

The limousine maneuvers into a narrow driveway at the side of the museum. As they enter the garage, Ted notices a well-dressed woman waiting by the curb. When the limo stops, Sally opens the door and reaches out to greet Ted, "Hello, my name is Sally Williams. I'm the Director of Contemporary Art. It's a pleasure to meet you."

"Hello," says Ted. "I do regret this morning's terrible incident."

"It's crazy. We really haven't had this much excitement since the Mapplethorpe exhibit a few years ago. That exhibit required double security," answers Sally.

Neil say, "I'm going to head back to my office and prepare for the press conference. Could you please show Professor Shearing around and fill him in on today's schedule?"

"Sure thing," says Sally. "Come this way, Professor Shearing. Your package arrived several days ago. After lunch, I'll show you the theatre, and you can prepare for your performance. Everyone is curious about the particular artwork that you will...uh...use in your performance."

"Well, I hope I can be somewhat entertaining after this morning's event."

Each performance on this road trip has been met with somewhat mixed reviews. Those who consider themselves as preservationists of art, even bad art, have expressed deep concerns over Ted's performances. Critics who never liked conceptual art are stymied, as Ted represents both what they like (i.e., to see conceptual art viewed as trash) and what they dislike (i.e., to see another stupid conceptual artist on the scene). Finally, there are those obnoxious, neophillic critics who think Ted's work initiates a new and exciting wave in creative expression. One admiring critic coined the phrase, "Terrorist Art," to describe the new style that Ted has initiated. In scholarly circles, Ted's performances raise provocative questions: How far do you go? Who determines what is valued? Does ownership of an art work permit one to destroy it? Can trash today be a prized piece tomorrow and vice versa? Is Ted a genius or a crazed psychotic?

At this moment in semi-darkness, Ted stands in a beautiful theatre at center stage behind a long table. He opens the cardboard box that Clare had shipped to the museum under Ted's instructions. Inside, he first fishes out a brand new blowtorch. In Denver, Ted had to resort to throwing matchsticks at the artwork when his blowtorch ran out of propane. This bit of improvisation flustered Ted, though the audience seemed pleased by the act.

Ted places the new blowtorch on the table, bends over, and retrieves the rest of his supplies: a can of lighter fluid, matches, and a work by up and coming New York artist Ben Hera. The artwork is rather small compared to others by Ben (and others that Ted has annihilated). Ben is known for his series of pieces made of animal skins. His abusive father was an avid hunter, and when Ben was a boy he was forced to shoot and trap animals of varying sizes, from rodents to fairly big game. His father trained Ben to skin the animals so he could display the pelts as rugs or wall hangings in their home. When his father died (rather unusually from a bacterial infection), Ben was left with dozens of animal pelts of various sizes and species. As a way of retribution and homage to the animals, Ben creates art with the skins.

State of the Arts

All of Ben's works are essentially the same. For each pelt, he removes the fur by carefully trimming and then shaving its entirety. After the fur is completely removed, he scrapes off as much of the subdermal tissue as he can and then uses solvents, such as hydrogen peroxide, to further thin and lighten the skin. After several chemical treatments, the animal pelt is reduced to a ghostly membranous film. Ben lightly tints these skins, which give them an eerie, translucent luster. Ben calls his series, "Minimal Animals," and they include such pieces as "Minimal Bear, "Minimal Moose," and "Minimal Beaver." Ted lifts from the package the artwork, which is entitled, "Minimal Mouse" or as Ted calls it, "Minnie Mouse." The piece is tinted blue and mounted like a decal onto a sheet of glass, which is surrounded by a metal frame. The piece has the appearance of a window pane with a bluish splotch in the center in the shape of road kill.

Ted places "Minnie Mouse" on the table next to his blowtorch, matches, and lighter fluid. He worries that his performance may not be as dramatic as it could be, given the backdrop of this morning's event. He walks around the table and looks at the piece from the perspective of the audience. Indeed, his display appears small and underwhelming, but it's too late to worry about it. Ted reaches into his canvas bag, and as he has done before each museum performance, takes a photograph of his setup with his camera.

As Ted makes his way back to Sally's office, he hears loud murmurs, forcing him to glance to his left. At the museum entrance, he sees a large crowd held in place by security guards. The officers allow in several TV crewmen who are carrying large cameras, lights, cables, and other video equipment. The noisy crowd is not at all like those who have attended Ted's previous performances. Indeed, they look more like featured guests on the "Jerry Springer Show." Behind the crowd is a white van with the logo "Eye On LA" painted on its side and a large satellite dish perched prominently on its roof.

Ted rushes back to Sally's office, as nervousness approaches total panic. Sally looks up from her desk and says, "It's going to be quite an afternoon. The story about the 'psychopathic artist,' as the press has called this morning's perpetrator, is the top news on all of our local stations. And look," Sally points to her computer screen, "you're on my Yahoo page!"

Ted bends over and squints at the monitor. He sees a photo of himself, one taken this morning at the airport, displayed next to a photo of a guy seated in a car, wearing a hooded sweatshirt, eyes transfixed, looking like the Unabomber on his way to the post office. "My God," he says, "I can't believe this."

"Have you looked outside? Looks like today's news brought out all sorts of weirdoes to the museum. I've never seen anything like this before. There's a guy dressed in a Renaissance costume. I guess he's supposed to be Leonardo…and there's another one with a goatee and bloody bandage around his head. It's going to be a real zoo." Sally's remark tumbles Ted to a point beyond panic.

Neil knocks on the open door and says, "Hi. It looks like we're ready. They're collecting tickets and allowing people into the theatre. I've called in extra security. Also, Ted, I managed to book an earlier flight back to San Francisco for you. The limo that I rented this morning will take you to the airport immediately after your performance. Take your suitcase to the room behind the stage and you can grab it up just before you leave. Sally will escort you to the door which will take you out to the garage. As the press is making this event a circus show, I figured the sooner you're away the better."

"Thanks so much," says Ted. "I'm truly grateful for your consideration and forethought."

"No problem," answers Neil. "We'll try to protect you, us, and art!"

With a few minutes before show time, Ted sits with Sally and Neil in a dark musty room behind the stage. Even with the stage door closed he can hear the crowd chanting, "WE WANT TED, WE WANT TED, WE WANT TED…"

Neil rises and says, "Well I guess we'd better get this thing started. Ted, I'll make a brief introduction and call you onto the stage."

As Neil opens the stage door, the sound of the crowd hits Ted, as if he's been transported to the center arena of a major event at the Coliseum (LA or Rome). A bright shaft of light, generously provided by TV crews, strikes the floor. Neil's large, silhouetted frame diminishes into the searing light as he moves toward center stage. The chants turn into boisterous screams as the crowd assumes Neil is Ted.

Neil moves toward center stage, picks up a small wireless microphone on the table and says, "May I have your attention, please." Without any change in the audience's sound level, Neil moves the microphone closer to his mouth and firmly says, "Please." As the noise begins to subside slightly, he continues, "Welcome, my name is Neil Sternum, and I'm the Director of the Museum."

With that statement, the crowd responds with, "WE WANT TED, WE WANT TED…"

"PLEASE!" Neil says with a stern voice. "Ted Shearing's

performance will begin in a minute. We, of course, did not expect such a large audience. This is an art performance, and I should warn you, it will be quite brief. During his performance, I must ask you to remain seated. As you know, Professor Shearing has developed an unusual form of performance art. For your protection, do not approach the stage, and please follow the directions of the security officers as you exit. And now, it is my pleasure to bring onto the stage, Ted Shearing."

With that cue, Ted gets up and walks timidly onto the stage toward Neil. Amidst the commotion, Neil clips the small microphone onto Ted's lapel and exits stage right.

Alone now, Ted looks up only to be blinded by the TV spotlights. Years of teaching haven't prepared him for this event. He clears his throat and mutters, "Hello."

With that remark, the crowd stamps their feet and yells, "TED, TED, TED, TED…"

Ted tries to continue, "I'm happy to be here and certainly do not condone this morning's events."

No one can hear him as the crowd's new mantra is, "BLOW IT UP, BLOW IT UP, BLOW IT UP…"

Ted forsakes the audio part of his performance. He grabs "Minimal Mouse" and lifts it over his head showing the crowd the sacrificial animal.

The crowd responds with cheers and more of "TED…TED…TED," which reverberates through the theatre. Ted puts the piece down and reaches for the can of lighter fluid. He squeezes the can and squirts out a fine spray, dousing the glass and the thin skin of "Minimal Mouse." Ted grabs the blowtorch and rotates the little screw near the nozzle, expecting a release of propane gas. He forgets, however, that in order to ignite a new blowtorch for the first time he needs to switch off a safety release. Unfortunately, with the noise of the crowd he can't tell if the blowtorch is hissing or not.

With mounting impatience, the crowd switches back to the "BLOW IT UP" chant.

After several unsuccessful attempts to light the blowtorch, Ted gives up and tosses a lighted matchstick onto "Minimal Mouse." Flames erupt from the glass, disintegrating the artwork in an instant. The flames, however, are barely visible due to the bright TV lights. Indeed, from the crowd's point of view, nothing has happened.

Ted steps back from the table and bows gallantly to the crowd, relieved that his performance is over. The crowd, as if witness to a poorly performed magic act, quiets for a moment, realizes that the show is over, then viciously turns on Ted. They erupt with loud boos and hisses.

Dumbfounded, Ted glances stage left and right. He notices the security officers fondling their holsters and looking nervously at each other. Through the bright lights, Ted peers out into the crowd, though unable to see much beyond the front row. He does notice the fellow dressed like Leonardo standing on his seat yelling and giving him the "thumbs down." Ted freezes in panic.

Fortunately, Neil steps up to the rescue. He removes the microphone from Ted's lapel and tells him that he should now leave and follow Sally to the garage. Ted, thankful for some guidance, runs off stage. He finds Sally standing nervously by his luggage. Ted picks up his suitcase and shoulder bag and hurriedly follows Sally down the hall and out the museum door. In the garage, a chauffeur stands by his limo, then takes Ted's suitcase and offers him the sanctity of his carriage.

Ted turns back and gives Sally a quick wave and "goodbye."

Sally waves back, relieved that Ted's rather disappointing performance is over.

Back in the theatre, the crowd jumps and screams: "WE WANT MORE, WE WANT MORE, WE WANT MORE…"

Exasperated, Neil puts the microphone to his mouth and says, "I'm sorry Ted Shearing has left…Ted is gone…the performance is over…Ted has left the building."

11

On a sweltering summer morning in Manhattan, Ben Hera sits comfortably behind the counter in the air-conditioned gift store of the New Works Art Institute. Two elderly women chat and caress silk scarves that lay on the counter. Other than Ben and these two women, the gift store is empty. While Ben casually thumbs through the current issue of *ARTNews*, he comes across an article about Ted's performance in Los Angeles. His mood moves from ho hum, to curiosity, to anger, and then beyond. Near the end of the article, Ben blurts "What the fuck!"

The two women, visibly shaken, mutter to each other, then skitter to the exit, giving Ben scathing looks. As Ben re-reads the article, he wonders: How could he be the subject of such ridicule? Weeks ago he heard of Ted's antics as the Anarchist of Art and expressed amusement at his performances. Yet Ben never imagined that he would the object of Ted's personal crusade against bad art. The article even suggests that the annihilation of "Minimal Mouse" was not a particularly sorrowful outcome.

Before this singular moment, Ben's career was rather typical for an aspiring young artist in New York City. His day job at the Institute's gift store gives him the opportunity to attend seminars for free, meet other artists, and keep abreast of the avant-garde. He shares a grungy flat in SoHo with his lover, Ivy, an artist who specializes in large macramé sculptures of female anatomy. Her two most famous pieces are "Twiny Twat" and "Untittied," the latter being a full-sized female nude made with knotted strands of rope. The title comes from the fact that there are holes where breasts should be. Ben and Ivy share a "studio" which is filled with rolls of rattan twine and boxes of animal pelts. They have lived together for almost a year. Ben's former partner, Jim, actually found the flat but left it and Ben for a traveling Brazilian musician. Ben's sexual orientation is rather mixed. He tends to alternate between male and female partners, but generally fantasizes about other species during intercourse.

Still seething, Ben's thoughts swirl in a confusion of murderous plots. The article notes that Ted will make an appearance in New York. He will perform next month at the illustrious Cunningham New Art Museum (known as CNew). Shotgun? Razor? Chemicals? Raccoon? With so many lethal possibilities at Ben's disposal, he tries to narrow his weapon of choice. Much like the game of *Clue*, he knows who but has to figure out where and how. In Ben's blurred mind, he feels he's not only representing all aspiring artists but also all forms of road kill and other disadvantaged animals who have been subject to annihilation by human hands. As he ponders over the possibilities, Ben fondles his lucky rabbit foot keychain nestled in his pants pocket.

Lunch approaches, and Ben is still steaming. He grabs his phone and calls Olympia, his friend and co-worker, "Hi, it's Ben. Sorry to call you up so early."

"Hi B, what's up?" asks Olympia.

"Can you fill in for me at the gift store this afternoon? I'm feeling awful. Maybe a flu or something but my stomach is acting up," says Ben not completely lying.

"Uh, I guess so. I should be able to get there to open up after lunch."

"Great. Thanks. I really appreciate it. I owe you one."

Ben locks up the gift store and heads toward the museum exit. He pulls on the door and lets the August heat and humidity pour over his face. He scurries onto the sidewalk, sweat already gathering around his collar. Without awareness, Ben finds himself walking up Fifth Avenue toward CNew. Like a hunter, he imagines himself in the woods, shotgun in hand, senses at full alert. Every cab and pedestrian passing by call him to action.

Ben rounds the corner. He spies the Corinthian columns that frame the entrance to CNew. A peculiar contradiction in form and content, CNew is housed in a Greek revival monstrosity. Ben hops up the steps, pulls hard on the heavy, ornate doors, and enters the museum. At the reception desk, a young woman sits dressed in standard avant-garde garb—black turtleneck, black pants, and heavy black mascara. Her fuzzy, rust-streaked hair and black rings around her eyes remind Ben of one of his pelts. Raccoon? He hands the receptionist a few dollars for admission and then asks, "Do you have a schedule of upcoming events?"

Without a word, the attendant moves her eyes down and to the right, fixating on the pile of pamphlets located further down the counter.

Ben, interpreting the nonverbal gesture, moves toward the pamphlets, picks up a schedule of events, and goes through a turnstile. As he scans the schedule, he suddenly bumps into a velvet rope that prevents him from forward advance. He looks up and sees a gigantic spiral of coiled metal that starts from his left, then arches far up and over to his right. The huge coil quivers in response to an air vent. The piece looks exactly like a gargantuan toy Slinky, and is entitled, "Spring in New York." Ben confronts this sculpture and wonders why CNew isn't interested in any of his pieces. His Minimal Animals are certainly more evocative and original than this piece of sheet metal.

Ben reads about Ted's upcoming performance, which will be held in the Delphi room. He moves slowly around the velvet rope, down the hall, and toward the gallery halls. He looks left and right, as if casing the joint. When he finds the Delphi room, he enters and sees in the center a white circular platform that apparently can be used as a small stage. Placed around the room and on the walls are various art pieces and odd looking sculptures. Just behind the stage stands a white plaster piece that looks exactly like Venus deMilo, only she has arms and a slightly perturbed expression. The arms are folded in front of Venus and her expression is one of sublime and absolute boredom.

On either side of Venus stands a thick marble column. As Ben approaches the statue, he notices three small speakers attached to the base of the stage. When he hops onto the stage, one of the speakers erupts with a loud, out of tune male voice singing "Row, row, row your boat…" Just after the voice sings "gently down the stream," a second speaker chimes in with the tune sung in the same terrible voice; and of course the duet is soon accompanied by a third voice emanating from the third speaker. As Ben stands in the middle of the stage, he is treated to several rounds of "Row, Row, Row Your Boat," in three-part contrapuntal disharmony.

Relieved when the "music" stops, Ben hops down from the

stage and moves around the room. He looks above, below, and to the sides, intently studying the room, though ignoring all of the art pieces around him. He returns to the front of the stage and imagines Ted at the center with blowtorch in hand and some poor artwork ready to be made art history. As if from some divine intervention, Ben is struck with an image, actually a moving picture, of Ted being blown up while he performs.

A chilly breeze from an over-enthusiastic air-conditioner hits Ben, though he is still sweating profusely. Excited, he hops back onto the stage, forgetting that this act initiates another boisterous round of "Row, Row, Row Your Boat." He kneels down and feels under the edge of the stage. There are no openings or compartments. He looks up at the marble columns, but they are smooth and non-descript. He then turns to Venus and stares salaciously at her from head to foot. She appears unperturbed, actually rather bored by Ben's advances. As Ben scans her physique, he notices a space between her waist and folded arms. Indeed, he thinks that there may be enough space there to conceal some kind of small explosive.

Energized by revenge, Ben quickly heads out the room, exits the museum, and scampers toward the nearby subway stop. In the train, rocking from side to side, Ben works out a scenario. He will find a way to plant explosives in the Delphi room before Ted's arrival. During the performance he will detonate it, thus performing his own artistic act. The plan does call for a bit of sophistication in bomb construction and detonation, but with Ben's knowledge of solvents and help from the internet, he feels he will be able to concoct a decent explosive device. Amid the clatter of the subway, Ben chuckles, pleased that Venus will be his accomplice.

Back at his flat, Ben opens the door and sees Ivy swinging in her homemade hammock. She is slim and completely nude, except for headphones and a tangle of twine coiled around her tummy. A small fan, clipped to the windowsill, blows her long, dyed jet-black hair to the side, as her toes move in rhythm to the unheard music. For a moment, she doesn't notice Ben and continues tying a series of twiny knots. When he shuts the door, Ivy looks over, removes her headphones, and says, "Hey, what's up?"

"Hi. I started feeling really nauseous at the museum. I dunno what it is. I called Olympia, and she's gonna fill in for me today. On my way back I began to feel a little better, but I'm still feeling queasy."

Ivy hops down from her perch, sets aside her knotted strands of twine, and slips into an oversized tie-dye t-shirt. She says, "Gee, want some tea?"

"Naw, I'm just gonna hang out, check my email and play on the computer."

"OK," she says, wrapping her thin arms around Ben and giving him a kiss. As she glances at the clock, she says, "Oh, I'm supposed to meet Diana at the Hermes Café. Actually right now. I gotta go. Will you be all right?"

"Yeah, sure. Don't worry, maybe it was just something I ate. Maybe the eggplant last night, I dunno."

Ben settles down in front of his computer as Ivy puts on a pair of cutoffs and sandals. She removes the t-shirt and dons a light muslin shirt with colorful designs embroidered around the collar. She takes a few seconds to brush her hair and then says, "OK, I'll see you. I'll be back in a few hours."

"OK, see you."

Ivy shuts the door behind her while Ben clicks into action. He types, "small plastic explosives," and hits the search button. He scans through the web listing, which displays a variety of paramilitary groups, construction companies, and survivalists. Interestingly, among the sites by redneck anarchists and demolition supply stores are mail order sites for plastic explosives from various former Soviet countries, such as Romania, Kazakhstan, and the Czech Republic. Ben is intrigued by these foreign websites but figures there won't be enough time to order something from the arsenal of former members of the Soviet bloc.

He changes his search and types "chemical explosives" and finds several sites with "recipes" for rather potent bombs. In fact, he finds a form of plastic explosive that he could probably concoct with chemical solvents, some of which he already has on his shelf. It appears that a gel-like explosive can be made that is compact, fairly stable, and rather potent.

As the printer spews out a chemical bomb recipe, Ben draws his attention to methods of detonation. Apparently, these explosives require a blasting cap that can be detonated by a small electrical spark. The trick will be to figure out a method of remote detonation. Ben types "remote bomb detonators," and finds a listing of fairly expensive devices. These detonators are equipped with wireless remotes that can be used at distances of up to a half mile. However, all of these devices are well beyond Ben's credit card limit.

Ben narrows his search to "cheap remote bomb detonators," and comes up with a handful of sites. The one that catches his eye is from *www.kill_your_neighbor.com.* It explains how a cell phone can be wired to detonate a blasting cap. The site includes schematics and detailed instructions for a small battery-powered device that, when initiated, will spark a blasting cap. It shows how to modify and attach a variety of popular cell phones to the device so that the blasting cap can be fired remotely when the perpetrator makes the critical call from another phone. For convenience, the site includes links to cheap pay-as-you-go cell phones. After a few clicks, Ben finds a suitably cheap cell phone and adds it to his virtual shopping cart. He does not opt for the extended warranty.

Ben grins fiendishly, amazed at how simple it will be to construct his homemade bomb. He can purchase his chemicals from the place where he usually gets his solvents and no one will think it odd. The little detonating device and cell phone rig will be easy to make. Ben can almost see the Delphi room at performance time, with Venus armed and Ted unaware of his demise. He thinks, 'What a fine piece of conceptual art' and unconsciously sings "Row, row, row your boat..."

12

One month later on another hot and humid day, Ted and Clare sit next to each other in a fake-leather booth eating breakfast across the street from their hotel on Times Square.

"Haven't been in New York in years. It's exciting, not scary as some think," says Ted, as he pours ketchup over his hash browns.

"Maybe we can catch a play tomorrow? What's your schedule like?" asks Clare.

"This evening we have the banquet and then the evening symposium. I get to moderate a discussion on 'Is Art Dead?' Tomorrow morning I have a discussion session with NYU students and that's it. I'm sure I'll be brain dead after that but I can perk up by the evening. Let's see if we can get tickets. There should be some time after my performance this afternoon to check out the possibilities."

"Great. It would be fun to spend a sabbatical here," says Clare. "Just think, we could get some writing done, go to the theatre, hit museums and enjoy the craziness of this city." Just as Clare finishes her outspoken thought, she realizes the seriousness of her faux pas.

"Yeah, well, you can take a sabbatical. As I'm currently unemployed, I don't have to worry about teaching, sabbaticals, and the rest of that academic crap," moans Ted.

As expected, Ted was fired from Napa State. The review committee unanimously agreed that Professor Shearing endangered his students and degraded the integrity of the college. A few close friends attended his "going away" party, though Ted was much too depressed to offer a performance after dinner. His friends sympathized and encouraged him to continue with his "art," though secretly most were dumbfounded by the incredible attention he has been getting from the art world. The most thoughtful gesture was made by Dave Connerly, who gave Ted a heart-warming going-away present—the Brett Weston photograph that they both had vied for on the internet. As a condition for receiving the gift, Ted had to promise not to blow it up.

"I'm sorry, love," says Clare. "That was insensitive. But you can still do the writing you've been wanting to do, and I'm sure the universities and museums around here would welcome you as an affiliate. Maybe even more now than before."

"Yeah, you're right," says Ted in a tone that is soft and loving. "It really would be fun for us to hang out in New York for a year."

Since his release from Napa State, Ted and Clare's relationship has grown considerably more intimate. Ted, with time on his hands to consider his future, invited Clare to live with him. Clare accepted, moved in, and rented her house. The living arrangement suits Kevin, as he now has a bigger bedroom, a bigger television, and a wider bandwidth for internet access. Practically speaking, the living situation has worked well for all, as Clare can save a decent amount of her salary for Kevin's college fund, and Ted doesn't have to worry about leaving his house unattended when he is out on the road, which has been rather frequent during the past several months. In fact, the honoraria garnered from his performances and lectures are nearly double his monthly salary as a tenured professor at Napa State.

Ted and Clare exit the restaurant, arms intertwined, and wade through the moist heat. They approach their hotel, push revolving doors, and enter the cool environs of air-conditioning. They cross the lobby and when they reach the elevators, Ted hits the up button. Ascending swiftly, Ted gives Clare a salacious grin. Clare responds with a surreptitious squeeze of Ted's unpublic area. Feeling the moment grow, Ted brings Clare close, moves his hands up her bare thighs, and gently kisses her.

When Ted hits her button, Clare yields a soft moanful sigh, then says, "Hey big boy, don't forget we're in a glass elevator."

By the time they enter their room, both are primed and ready. Ted hangs the "Do Not Disturb" sign and turns around to see Clare's lusty trail of sandals, summer shorts, t-shirt, lacy bra and wet panties, which leads directly to a sprawled and eager Clare, her internal temp as hot and moist as the weather outside.

"We'd better start moving. We need to meet the museum people for lunch in an hour," says Ted, arms around Clare in post-hedonistic bliss.

Clare arches up, flings rumpled sheets, and says, "guess so," and saunters nakedly over to the bathroom.

Ted yells, "Do you think I should wear my maroon or blue tie?"

"How 'bout the maroon one," Clare yells just before turning on the shower.

Ted, in boxer shorts, irons his shirt and mentally rehearses his performance. As this is his most prestigious engagement to date, he certainly doesn't want to "bomb." After the fiasco in Los Angeles, Ted has refined his act. He commissioned his colleague Ed Sparta, the metalwork artist, to customize foolproof trashcans for his performances. These trashcans are truly works of art. Ed welded clamps near the top of a trashcan so that the lid can be secured and withstand the pressure of a Red Devil. He also drilled a hole in the center of the lid large enough for Ted to drop a firecracker down its gullet. All around the sides smaller holes were drilled which act to alleviate pressure when the firecracker explodes. After several test versions, some of which have marred Ed permanently, an almost perfectly safe contraption was built.

The customized trashcan has never failed during a performance, though Ted is still billed exorbitantly for hazard insurance and for a rented bulletproof Plexiglas barrier. In fact, Ted's performance budget just about equals his honorarium earnings. He really doesn't care, as he is devoted to his art. Indeed, Ted's bedroom walls are now adorned with a photographic history of his performances. He had each of his pre- and post-performance shots placed together in a frame and arranged in chronological order. Thus, starting from his bed and moving to the right, one can see Ted's history as an artist, from his crude beginning with help from Jonathan Smead to his most current, well-crafted performances courtesy of Ed Sparta.

Ted's last six performances have proceeded in exactly the same and well-received manner. Working in dim lighting, Ted drenches an artwork with lighter fluid, places it into its final resting place, and clamps the lid. With skillful aplomb, acquired through practice, he lights up a Red Devil and drops it into the abyss. After a nervous moment, a harsh yellow flame bursts from the large hole on the lid, and at the same time, tiny flashes of light poke out like sun rays from the smaller holes around the trashcan. This extravaganza is accompanied by a muted blast followed by a big black puff of smoke which shoots up toward the ceiling with a wonderfully swirling trail. Finally, tiny jet streams of smoke shoot out of the smaller holes. The audience, slightly stunned yet thoroughly impressed, gives Ted an uproarious round of applause. Ted graciously bows, points to the now bloated and smoldering trashcan, and in his mind thanks the genius of Ed's metalwork.

"Will you hook my bra?" asks Clare, who really doesn't need Ted's help but wants to shake him from his deep thoughts.

"Sure," says Ted, taking lecherous advantage of her before he helps out, which was pretty much what Clare expected.

"I hope it won't be too boring at lunch," remarks Clare.

"You never look bored," responds Ted, "In fact, whenever we have dinner with people, I look across the table and you're engaged in lively conversation with some person. Whether it's a handsome dude or some old fart, you have a super ability to listen and converse."

"Well, maybe it's because I hang around clinical psychologists. They're trained to listen," says Clare, though in actuality she has a natural knack of listening and making others feel comfortable. Of course, her youthful looks and engaging smile works wonders with both handsome dudes and old farts.

Dressed for success, Ted and Clare exit the cool confines of the hotel and enter the garish environs of Times Square, with its flashing video screens, now glimmering flaccidly in the late-morning sun. They hail a taxi and weave their way to the Cunningham New Art Museum.

Over the blather of a talk radio personality jabbering about the covert infiltration of terrorists in New York City, Ted asks Clare, "Will you marry me?"

Clare—and Ted—are both stunned by this out-of-the-blue remark. Clare's first thought, which almost reaches her larynx, is, 'What made you say that?' However, she regroups, then says, "What a surprise, Ted, of course I'll marry you!"

As they embrace, both are stunned and perplexed, especially Ted, who says, "I'm just as surprised as you, but you know, it seems right right now."

Clare, not knowing exactly what Ted means, smiles, caresses his cheeks, and murmurs, "I love you."

As Ted echoes the remark, the taxi driver, oblivious to what's happening in the back seat, pulls sharply into the no parking zone in front of the Cunningham New Art Museum.

With newfound excitement for the future, Ted and Clare leave the cab and head up the stairs of CNew. About halfway up, Ted says, "Hold on a minute, I want to take a photograph of the entryway." He pulls his camera out of his shoulder bag, frames a shot, and takes a shot.

In a moment, the two are in CNew. At the reception desk, Ted approaches the morose, raccoon-faced receptionist, says his name and what he is here for. Without a word, the young woman picks up the phone, mutters into the mouthpiece, hangs up, looks up and glances to the left. Unfortunately, Ted is perplexed as he is not as well-versed in nonverbal animal communication as Ben Hera. However, Clare is and pulls Ted to the marble bench to wait.

After a few moments, a gentleman stuffed into an olive green suit, makes his way towards Ted and Clare. With a porcine grin, the man extends his thick hand toward Ted, and announces, "Hello, Mr. Shearing, I'm Clark Compote, museum director."

Ted grasps Clark's warm, sweaty paw and says, "Hello Clark, this is my, uh...fiancée, Clare Singer.

"Nice to meet you, Clare," says Clark as he shakes her hand.

Ted adds, "It's a real pleasure to be here."

"For me too," says Clark. "What I mean to say is that I've just relocated from the Chicago area. I was director of the Evanston Art Museum. I was hired here by CNew a few months ago. The previous director was fired. You know, with drastic cuts in revenue and donations over the past several years, museums all over have been hurting. I have a MBA from Loyola and was once an avid art collector, so I'm here to try to turn things around...but enough about me, how was your trip?"

"So far, it's been wonderful. I've forgotten how exciting New York can be," answers Ted.

Extending his arm toward the hallway, Clark says, "Let me take you to our small luncheon room. We're just about ready to be served."

Clark leads the way and passing the Delphi room he says, "This is where your performance will be held."

The Delphi room looks much as it did a month ago when Ben Hera visited, except for the steel table on the stage, the rows of chairs, and the Plexiglas barrier placed between the stage and front row. Upon much closer inspection, one could detect the nearly imperceptible white package concealed under Venus' left elbow, which contains a small cell phone and homemade bomb.

"Very nicely arranged," says Ted.

The group continues down to the end of the hall to an elevator. Clark pushes the "up" button and, after a short wait, takes Ted and Clare up to the fourth floor. With glowing memories of their past elevator ride, Ted grins at Clare, while she squeezes Ted's hand in mock stimulation.

They exit the elevator and go through a glass door that says "Staff Only Area." They walk through a maze of white cubicles, stopping occasionally as Clark introduces Ted and Clare to various staff members.

Through another door, quite modern in style, Clark guides Ted and Clare into a dark room paneled with mahogany. Flowing velvet curtains block most of the sunlight attempting to enter the room. Around a heavy oak table in the middle of the room, sits a group of well-dressed individuals conversing in rapid, vapid chatter. The group at once looks up, quiets, and smiles at the new arrivals.

Clark announces, "May I introduce you all to our guest artist, Ted Shearing, and his fiancée, Clare Singer."

The two men sitting at the table stand to greet the guests. One of them says, "Pleased to meet you. I'm Sam Cunningham, welcome to the museum," Sam, who is short, bald, and impotent, directs his hand toward a frumpy woman sitting across the table and says, "This is my wife, Betty." Sam knows absolutely nothing about contemporary art and views his inherited collection much as Ted views his own collection. It is Betty, in her a brightly colored dress and coiffed with red-dyed hair, who views herself as the connoisseur of fine art and the next Peggy Guggenheim.

Smiling, Betty stands and says, "We're all excited to meet you. Please sit down." She directs Ted to the head of the table and Clare to the other end.

Next to Clare stands a handsome, fiftyish gentleman who smiles, shakes Clare's hand, glances at Ted, and says in an affected, Clark Gable intonation, "Hello, I'm Frank Farr."

At the sound of the name, Ted immediately has a flashback memory of a graduate seminar in a dusty classroom at Berkeley, listening to old Professor Whitehall speaking highly of the renowned New York University scholar, Frank Farr, famous for his stunning analysis of post-modernist theory. Ted recalls the moment as if it were yesterday: he is noticeably aroused, sitting in behind the beautiful Jennifer Langley and mentally stroking her long neck and blond hair. Whitehall inanely jabbers on about Farr's new volume, "Significant Signifiers."

Returning to the here and now, Ted says, "Well it's a pleasure to meet you, Professor Farr. I have fond memories of a graduate seminar in which we discussed your work."

"Call me Frank. I'm pleased that you've encountered my work." In a supercilious tone Frank asks, "Were you moved?"

Ted suppresses a grin and says, "Quite."

Clark squats down in the remaining empty seat. He swipes sweat from his forehead with one palm and motions with his other towards a women seated next to Ted and says, "Oh, and let me introduce you to Canoga Parks, who is one of our in-resident artists this year."

Canoga smiles and says, "Hello."

"You have an interesting name," says Ted.

"Yeah, I'm supposed to be one-sixty-fourth Indian."

Seated on the other side of Canoga is Sam, who lasciviously eyes her long neck and black hair. Sam adds, "Canoga makes movies."

"Actually, I create digital videos," quips Canoga, who subtlety but explicitly turns away from Sam and toward Ted.

"Interesting," says Ted, "I have some digital works in my art collection. I also did my doctoral thesis on film. What sort of work do you do?"

"Well I was selected by CNew for my portfolio on suburban

life. I grew up in Southern California, and these days whenever I visit my parents I set up my camera and keep it running for up to a couple of hours in auto mode. I shoot at places like street intersections, shopping malls, and playgrounds. I edit the stuff I like. CNew was impressed by my water works, my close-up videos of sprinklers and gutters."

"Hmm, sprinklers, that's interestingly odd," says Ted. He ponders for a moment, then ventures a question, "Have you ever heard of a piece called 'Rainbird in Motion'?"

"Wow, that's weird," says Canoga. "That's my ex-boyfriend's video. When I first got to New York, we met and hung out for a while. I was really pissed when he came home with that clip as it was a direct rip-off of my own stuff. He wasn't even into sprinklers before he met me. He was filming horseshit around Central Park. Even worse, 'Rainbird' won a prize."

Ted thinks to himself: Well, it's history now. He utters, "I'd love to see your work," perhaps a little more flirtaceous than he should have.

On the other side of the table, Frank Farr says to Clare, "You might like to see my collection, though as a psychologist I shudder to think how you might interpret it."

"Well, I'm not that kind of psychologist," says Clare. "What do you collect?"

"Well," says Frank, "My scholarly work has centered around found art and ready-mades, you know, Duchamp, Rauschenberg, and more contemporary artists. I've explored the theoretical underpinnings of their work. But exquisite museum pieces are way beyond my budget, so instead I spend a lot of my spare time at dumps around town and in New Jersey. I collect toilet seats and hang then on my walls at home and in my office."

"You're right. Freud would have a field day with you, but remember, I'm engaged to a man who expresses himself with firecrackers."

Conversation continues as the guests are treated with a fine five-course meal. After dessert and coffee, Clark glances at his watch and rises, scattering bread crumbs that were peacefully perched on his stomach. He says, "Well, it's about time we let Ted go and prepare his performance. Thank you all for coming."

With that remark, the group rises, makes friendly gestures of farewell, and exits the luncheon room, leaving Clark, Clare, and Ted behind.

After a brief call on his cell phone, Clark turns to Ted and says, "I've just asked security to move your materials from our storage room to the Delphi room. It should get there at about the same time we do."

"Great," says Ted. "That'll give me plenty of time to set up."

The three retrace their steps out the staff area. As they descend down the elevator, Clare says to Ted, "Maybe while you're setting up how 'bout I call some theatres and see if we can get tickets for a show tomorrow night?"

"Good idea," says Ted.

"What's your preference, comedy, musical, or artsy-fartsy?"

Ted gives his usual response, "Anything but science fiction."

When they reach the Delphi room, Clark greets a security guard standing by the entryway and says to Ted, "This is Tom. He will be here until the end of your performance. I've got to do some other things now, but I'll be back in a half hour or so. If you need anything, just ask Tom, and he'll get a hold of me."

"OK, thanks." Ted enters the quiet room and takes in the atmosphere. From the rear, he sees the rows of empty chairs, the

Plexiglas barrier, a large cardboard box on the stage next to the table, and Venus, who is, unknown to him, primed for action. A twinge of nervousness stirs his stomach as he imagines himself onstage with the crowd watching him.

Ted walks around the Plexiglas barrier and onto the stage. He opens the box and retrieves his materials, the customized trash can, lighter fluid, Red Devil, matches, and the artwork. Today's honored piece is by Hans deWied and is entitled "MOMA Lisa." Hans has made his reputation by purchasing fine art reproductions at the same museums where the originals are displayed. These reproductions are mounted and placed in simple black metal frames. Amazingly, a deWied hangs in many contemporary art museums. "MOMA Lisa" is the most popular (deWied has made dozens using the same image), but his works also include, "MOMA Goya, "MOMA Monet," and "MOMA Anonymous." Hans' works are among the most frequently viewed pieces at museums, as of course, many visitors think they are seeing a true Leonardo, Goya, Monet, or Anonymous.

The "MOMA Lisa" leans against the table onstage. Ted grabs his camera and moves in front of the table to take his pre-performance shot.

Satisfied with his setup, Ted grabs the large cardboard box and drags it to the back of the room. When he reaches the entryway, he says to Tom, "I'm done setting up. Where's a good place to put this box?"

Tom says, "Just leave it here and I'll get someone to remove it. In about 15 minutes, we'll begin seating."

"Great. I guess I'll stroll around the museum. I'll be back in a few minutes."

Ted heads out and looks for Clare. As he maneuvers around

the slinky, "Spring in New York," he sees her standing near the reception desk with cell phone in hand. When he sidles up to her, she smiles and gives him a thumbs up.

After a few moments, she hangs up and says, "Well I thought about a few things, 'Phantom,' a new production of 'Hedda Gabler,' but I ended up getting tickets for an off-Broadway play called 'The State of the Arts.' It's supposed to be fun and artsy."

"Sounds fine." Looking at his watch, Ted says, "We've got about 20 minutes. Wanna walk around and help me stay calm?"

"Sure."

As Clare and Ted re-enter the museum halls, they pass by a fellow sitting on the marble bench by the reception desk. He is dressed in black, staring at a book in one hand while fondling a rabbit foot in the other.

It is, of course, Ben Hera, who nervously awaits his own artistic performance. He views his murderous act as an exquisitely creative work that expresses his feelings in a post-modern world. Unfortunately (or fortunately), he expects his performance (and assassination) to remain anonymous.

Last week, Ben's arming of Venus deMilo was exceedingly simple. He found plenty of time when the Delphi room was vacant, and the explosive device fit snugly under Venus' elbow. The only hitch was that Ben did not have the opportunity to test his detonating device, though he meticulously followed the instructions outlined at *www.kill_your_neighbor.com*. The clever device uses the vibration mode of a cell phone to place a wire in contact with a terminal, thus initiating a little spark that ignites a bigger spark from the blasting cap, that leads to an even bigger bang from the plastic explosives. Now, all Ben has to do to begin his artistic performance is push the auto dial button on the cell phone that is comfortably resting in his pants pocket.

Ben continues to wait, pretending to read his book. He tries calming himself but the jerky fondling of his rabbit foot and his own shaking leg reveal his true disposition. Every few minutes he glances at his watch and looks toward the Delphi room. About ten minutes past Ted's scheduled performance time, Ben hears a loud applause. He gets up and walks hesitantly down the hall. He doesn't enter the room. Instead he walks past, noticing that the room is nearly filled. There are even people standing in the back of the room. It pleases Ben that so many people have come to witness his performance. He strolls down the hall trying not to look as if he's about to murder Ted Shearing.

Ted, having just been introduced, stands proudly onstage. He holds MOMA Lisa in his hands and raises it above his head for display. As is usually the case at this point, members of the audience cheer for the sacrificial item. Clare sits in the front row in the reserved VIP section along with Clark, Sam and Betty Cunningham. Also in the front row are Frank Farr and Canoga Parks.

Ben reverses his stroll and makes his final pass by the Delphi room. He takes a quick glance into the room and sees Ted squirting lighter fluid into the trashcan. The audience waits in nervous anticipation. Sweating profusely now, Ben has the desire to rush, even run, out of the museum; but he works desperately to slow his pace. He looks robotic, erratically trying to hurry and slow down at the same time. He heads out the building, oblivious to the near 100% humidity that hits him, and then runs almost tripping down the steps. When he reaches the sidewalk, he stops, takes the cell phone out of his shirt pocket and with a shaking, nervous finger, presses the auto dial button.

At the same moment, Ted holds a just-lit Red Devil, its fuse sparkling near his fingertips. He quickly drops the firecracker into the trashcan. Yet before it actually explodes, Venus deMilo violently erupts. A powerful explosion follows and all hell breaks loose.

The cinema version of this episode depicts in silent, super slow motion the blast emanating from Venus's left elbow, and for a brief moment the sculpture looks exactly like the unarmed version that stands in the Louvre. Yet the next moment, Venus' upper torso is pulverized into bits, which splay out in all directions. When the force of the blast reaches Ted, he is lifted, arms extended in graceful slowness toward the Plexiglas barrier. To his side, the trashcan slowly tumbles forward along with Ted, and as it falls the Red Devil's now-exceedingly impotent blast erupts. Panning to the crowd, the camera shows unregistered expressions that slowly turn into puzzlement, shock, then ghastly horror. They view the explosion safely from behind the Plexiglas barrier, which gives the impression of a widescreen TV tuned to a segment of "Amazing Accidents Captured on Video."

Back in real time, horrific screams echo the room as the crowd rushes out to escape what appears to be a terrorist attack. Tom, the security guard, has already called 911 and helps guide people out. His desperate cries for everyone to be calm are drowned by the crowd's hysteria. In the melee, a women crouches on the floor near the entryway covering her face with her arms in hopes surviving the stampede. With dust and plaster still floating, Clare and Frank, now the only ones near the front, rush around the Plexiglas barrier. They find Ted, unconscious, slumped, lying limp against the base of the Plexiglas.

Frank warns, "Clare, don't move him. Let's wait for the paramedics."

Clare grabs Frank, hysterically shaking and cries, "Do you

think he's dead?"

"I don't know, but if his spinal cord is injured, you don't want to move or touch him. It could make it worse."

"Oh, my God," wails Clare through uncontrolled sobs.

Ted lies motionless; a trickle of blood dribbles out his nose and down his face.

13

Rejoice! riverruns, past streaming flyoes of unconscious flies fishing orynewk items, graspyng, lapsing onto horsey shyores along the ventral path. Synaptic underground...bottom-up graffiti...mind the gap...mind, the gap. Noisy mush-bryne Hebbnets spin unsharp masks over sulcal fjords. Peekshift peaks on occipital loaves yeasting hazily. I can CNew but Kant over calcarine ridges, whereas orbital nostrils sniffed, snuffed, stuffed with scrambled tofu on cribiform plate. Operator, can you help me place this call...

Ammon's horn sprouts over Madeline's bake shoppe, as we recall a weak end, and Derrida's d'arse is unconsoled. Sais what? Hippo on campus encode colorful seahorses signaling damn ampa, relationally bound and primed for the seas on H. M.'s ship, explicitly declaring Mnemo in hobknobbin' days, Arthurian tales searching for the golden engram. A long, long time ago, I can still remember...

Emo-thebigoneorfive of the HPA axis force war on angry aryans making 911 incalls. On an insular landscape, putrid turds hang on amputated arms of Venysdemilo revealing disembowled digestives trailed by Buneullian ants. Wee peons of Sam's dystruction...we demand shrubbery! A taste of the rats! Let's party and lick creamy cones with colorful balling loons and spunky funkyducks. Stop, in the name love...

It's snot art (aesthetically speaking). Where? Up a tree (cortically speaking). What? Embodied Ted (cognitively speaking). How? ISEM (theoretically speaking). Lights outs, cameras on, action! Manhattan project. Inmee wombe a dreame, inmee roome a bombe, inmee adobe an image with layers, channels, levels, history. I burn, I dodge, I adjust, I heal, I sharpen. It's not art, it's not art, it's not art, it's art, it's art, it's art, it's art, but so what? The pale end or the bucket of art. Is the trashcan half full or half empty? Dented? Art undaunted too? CNew butes, steub, subet, ebuts, ubets...tubes! Suren, renus, usner, esrun, neusr...nurse! Who I am? Ted I am. Dead I am? Scrambled brain and man I am. By the time I get to Phoenix, he'll be rising...

Ted opens his eyes and mutters, "Cogito ergo alive."

"Looks like Ted's 'wake," says Joyce, the attending nurse, removing a blood pressure cuff from Ted's arm.

Clare is asleep, curled up in a recliner. She opens her eyes slowly, climbs into consciousness, and utters, "Huh? What did you say?"

Ted's climb into consciousness will be much more difficult, like scaling Half Dome. He says again softly, "Cogito ergo alive."

Joyce checks the blinking monitor, "His heart rate is stable. Throughout the night, he's been muttering and moving. That's a good sign. What did he say?"

"I think he said 'Cogito ergo alive,' which would mean 'I think, therefore I'm alive,' which I guess is sort of cute and suggests some mental ability."

"Sounds like gibberish to me, but I'm no intellectual," says Joyce.

Clare leans over toward Ted, pilots her arm around bundles of wires and IV tubes, strokes his cheek, and says, "Hi darling, how are you?"

Ted stares, fixated on the ceiling, his brain wallowing in penury, no sense. Lines, sounds, pain, thirst. He turns toward Clare, slowly focuses, and sees a glazed, sugary torus smelling of sweet yeast attached to a rather lovely neck. "Krispy Kreme!" he says with loving excitement.

Clare, shocked by the response, reflexively retracts her hand from Ted's cheek.

"You must understand," says Joyce, "For a while he will act very strange and confused. It happens to a lot of patients right after a head injury. At least he's conscious now, though he might go in and out for a while. For you, the worst part is now, during the first days after his coma."

Clare slowly returns her hand to Ted's face, as a tear trails down her cheek. She caresses his shoulder, trying to decipher his unblinking expression. She smiles and says, "Hey, big guy, how're you doing?"

Ted stares at Clare. His brain strains, pushing the envelope in hopes of finding a message inside. He smiles back at Clare, sensing her loving warmth but not much else.

"Dr. Cartwright will be in this morning making the rounds," says Joyce. "She'll come by and talk to you. I'm done here, if you need help, just hit the call button."

"OK, thanks."

Ted blinks. His eyes move slowly around the room, as if viewing an alien planet. Nothing is familiar. He wiggles his fingers, jiggles his toes, and begins to hum, "It's a small world after all..." Apparently, the most rudimentary aspects of Ted's mental capacities start to emerge from a neuronal fog.

An hour later, a slender woman enters the room dressed in a white medical coat, her name sewn on her left breast pocket, with the proverbial stethoscope draped around her neck. Otherwise she is smartly attired, both physically and mentally. Dr. Karen Cartwright, young star of the Neurology ward, walks around Ted's bed and over to Clare. At first, Clare doesn't notice Dr. Cartwright's entry; she's sitting in the recliner, cradling a cup of coffee and reading the *New York Times*. Clare looks up, swivels her legs around to stand, but Dr. Cartwright gently places her hand on Clare's shoulder and says, "Please don't bother getting up. You must be exhausted. I'm Dr. Cartwright. Dr. Mandel, the physician you've been seeing, talked to me about Ted's case, and we've been going over his status."

"Please to meet you." says Clare. "How is Ted doing?"

Dr. Cartwright seats herself in an empty chair. She and Clare look over at Ted, who slumbers quietly. "Ted's vital signs have been stable for over 24 hours. His breathing and heart rate are normal, and I'm confident that he'll pull through. He was lucky not to have broken any bones. His spinal cord is intact, and skull x-rays don't show any cracks or fissures. But, I'm sure you know, Ted suffered a very serious head injury. Joyce mentioned that he appeared to be coming around last night, moving and coughing, and I guess he started talking this morning?"

"Yes, though he said some strange things."

"Well, for now it's good that he's coming around. The length of time in coma is often an indicator of how severe his brain injury is. I understand that you are a professor of psychology?"

"Yes, at Napa State College near San Francisco."

"I know the area. I grew up in Marin County and went to UCSF for med school. I've been by Napa State but never visited. Some high school friends of mine went there. I ended up at UC San Diego for college. I took some psychology courses there. In fact, one course really turned me on to neurology."

Clare contributes, "In grad school, I studied animal behavior. I do teach a little about brain injury in my introductory class, but I don't know much about the medical side of neurology."

"Well, one thing I learned in med school is that brain injuries in real life are never quite as clear-cut as those cases you read in textbooks. At least with medical advances these days, we are able to diagnose brain injuries better than before. I can show you Ted's MR scans…would you'd like to see them?"

"Sure," says Clare.

"Good. Come on over to my office. You can bring your coffee."

Clare follows Dr. Cartwright out the room and down the hall. Behind the nurses' post, Dr. Cartwright unlocks her office door, directs Clare to a rolling desk chair and sits in another one directly in front of a computer with a large, widescreen monitor. She rapidly taps on the keyboard, hitting the return key every so often. She pauses, and in a few seconds several brain images appear on the screen. She turns to Clare and says, "So here are Ted's scans."

Clare moves closer and sees a set of MRI scans of Ted's brain, though to Clare they simply look like an oval filled with splotches of light and dark areas.

Dr. Cartwright points and says, "These are images of Ted's brain as if you're looking down on his head. Here's the front of his head. Each scan is taken at various levels, from the lowest scan here, to the highest scan here. You can see the skull, and here are his ventricles."

Clare nods, indicating some but limited comprehension. "Do you see any brain damage?"

"Well, yes." Pointing to various spots on the scan, Dr. Cartwright continues, "At this time we see some brain swelling, as indicated here and here, and some hemorrhaging here and here. From what we can ascertain, when Ted hit that Plexiglas barrier, he damaged his frontal lobes, which is his most significant problem. When he fell, he also hit his head on the floor, which we think caused more damage in the back part of his brain."

"It looks really bad," says Clare, trying to stifle tears.

"The damage looks worse now because there's bleeding and swelling. It's good that Ted regained consciousness, though two days in a coma is rather severe. In many ways, he is very lucky. This kind of head injury, which we see often severe car accidents, usually results in a cracked skull and broken bones."

"What's his prognosis?"

"Ted may act rather odd and confused over the next few weeks, but I guarantee you, he will show significant recovery during the next several months. Given what I can see from his MR scans, Ted should pull through but he is likely to have long-lasting effects from this injury. We won't know for certain how much he will recover. But, as I say, he will show great improvement."

Walking back to Ted's room, Clare asks, "Do you think he'll be so bad that he'll need to be hospitalized forever?"

"No. His vital signs look good. We'll keep him here for a couple weeks and monitor the initial stages of recovery, and then he can go home. Depending on his mental disposition when he's released, he may or may not need home care. I understand that Ted recently left academia to pursue his art. I don't know about this stuff but friends of mine say that he has been quite a celebrity this year."

"Yes, Ted's been traveling around a lot giving performances, though this is only the second time I've seen him perform in public. This New York appearance was the biggest one to date. I'm not much into this art stuff myself, but he has been so excited about it. He has certainly been getting lots of enjoyment from all the notoriety."

"I've been fielding phone calls from reporters asking about Ted's status." Entering Ted's room, Dr. Cartwright notices Clare's *New York Times* on the table. She continues, "You should look at the *Arts* section in today's paper. There's a story about Ted's accident. I should warn you, though, they make a big point about the irony of his accident with respect to his performances. Also, the police are stymied. They figure that there are so many crazed artists and psychopaths in New York City that the chances of finding the perpetrator are slim."

Clare plops herself down on the recliner feeling the gravity of Ted's injury. She looks up at Dr. Cartwright and says, "On the way to the museum, before his performance, Ted proposed to me. It seems like such a long time ago."

"Will you be able to stay here in New York while Ted recuperates?"

"I think so, if it's only a couple of weeks. My ex-husband can take care of our son. I've been thinking that I may take a sabbatical for the upcoming year. I'm due for one, and then I can take care of Ted when we get home."

"That would be great. He'll benefit from having you around, and, as I said, he'll show significant recovery over the next several months. Keep in mind, for the next few days he probably won't be very coherent, but talk to him and try to communicate. I'll be checking in on him and so will Dr. Mandel. Also, when you get back to the Bay Area, you should contact Dr. Anthony Kingsley. He was my mentor at UCSF and is one of the best neurologists in the country. He's retired now and lives near Sonoma. He's always willing to help me out in cases like Ted's in which there's frontal lobe involvement." Grinning, Dr. Cartwright reveals, "Everyone called him 'King,' which was fitting as he was the world's leader in neurological science. Do you remember that singer, Prince? He changed his name to 'The Artist Formerly Known as 'Prince'? In med school, the students gave King a plaque that honored him as "The Neurologist Formerly Known as King." We still correspond via email. If you want, I'll send him a note and let him know about Ted's case."

"I would appreciate it. Thank you very much."

Dr. Cartwright exits, leaving Clare to think about the future, and Ted to think about anything he can.

14

"Door's ajar
Cool breeze with spring leaves
That won't settle."

"That's nice, Ted," answers Clare from the kitchen table. She taps on her laptop and says, "I'm going to add that one to your collection."

"Okie Dokie, Karaoke," says Ted, who squats low and peers through his camera, which is perched atop a tripod, angled and aimed at the rear door of his house.

During the months since his accident, Ted's crawl from mental oblivion has progressed in interesting and remarkable ways. At first, his sensory world was stripped of meaning. Lines, colors, shapes, and sounds registered, but Ted couldn't compose coherent pictures or thoughts. He would blurt out odd fragments from memory, as if his brain were testing the links between mind and body. Clare, along with immense patience, Dr. Cartwright, and the nurses, facilitated Ted's recovery by listening, chatting, and engaging him in what mostly were one-way social interactions.

Without much to do, Clare had Kevin ship her laptop to the hospital. She tried to work on research projects, but without articles and her animal behavior data, working was hopeless. She dabbled at a mystery novel, but fatigue and sadness prevented creative juices from stirring. Finally, Clare took to writing a chronicle of her feelings and of Ted's odd behavior. She ended up writing pages of entries, which gave her a way of coping and also offered a rather interesting characterization of Ted's recovery.

Near the end of their stay, Ted began to acknowledge the world. He performed his first meaningful act at three in the morning, an event symbolically marked by an exceedingly bright flash of light. When Clare opened her eyes, she saw Ted smiling in the dim afterglow, peering through his camera, its lens pointed at some twisted wires connected to his heart rate monitor. This first post-injury photograph marked the beginning of an incredible series of images taken by Ted during his recovery.

"Will you be ready to go soon?" asks Clare from the kitchen. "We need to head off in about a half an hour. We have a busy day with your appointment with Dr. Kingsley and the reception."

"Oakily Dokily." As demonstrated by Ted's absent-minded phraseology, his tray table is not quite in the full upright and locked position. His telegraphic speech and homage to pat phrases resemble his abridged thoughts. He manages to comprehend a decent amount and can converse, despite the economy of utterances. In fact, Clare's chronicle of Ted's quirky use of phrases and metaphors documents his remarkable recovery. Ted mainly speaks in odd rhythms and allusions, which seem almost poetic. Even Kevin finds interest in Ted's remarks. He and Jenny often sit and chat with Ted just to hear his colorful aphorisms. They feel Ted's quips, expressed primarily in haiku form, to have an inscrutable, Eastern quality to them. Kevin often jokes and tells Ted that he is the new Confucius. Ted responds by saying, "No, I'm Kung Fused."

Kevin backs the car slowly down the driveway and says, "OK, here we go." Last week, Kevin passed his driving test, and Clare has kept two promises: 1) letting Kevin drive her Volvo on occasion and 2) letting everyone else know via email that Kevin is now a legal driver. Interestingly, this rite of passage implanted a newfound sense of responsibility in Kevin.

Jenny sits next to Kevin while Clare and Ted hold hands in the back. Jenny turns in her seat and asks Ted, "So what do you think about Kevin's driving ability?"

"Teenage lust, hoping to stay alive through spring, with airbags," answers Ted. The others chuckle.

"You're doing really well, Kev," says Clare. "I'm impressed that you're being so careful. I'm proud of you."

"Thanks, mom."

"By the way Ted, thanks for this." Jenny holds up a large book. "Your prints are so interesting. I'm really looking forward to the reception."

The book is mostly Clare's doing. In her self-appointed role as Ted's art agent, she contacted Eugenia Beardsley, owner of the Inside Out Art Gallery in downtown Sonoma. Eugenia opened the place five years ago in honor of her son, Jeremy, who is mentally impaired, yet has a knack for finger painting. Jeremy has a permanent display, and other artists with "special" (read "mentally-challenged") abilities have had exhibitions at the Inside Out. Clare visited the gallery last year and showed Eugenia a portfolio of Ted's prints. Clare also read from her chronicle of Ted's recovery, which included many of his haiku-like descriptions of his photography. Eugenia was so impressed by both the prints and the "poetry" that she immediately offered a solo exhibition of Ted's photography. Clare's efforts have garnered today's catered reception and the large photo book of Ted's images which Jenny proudly holds in her hands.

Thumbing through the book, Jenny says, I really like your close-up photos."

"Beached kelp, tossed by summer surf, waits for more."

"I think it's incredible what Ted has accomplished since his accident," adds Clare. "His gallery exhibition just opened last Saturday, and he's already sold three prints! You know the first image that he took at the hospital, the one he calls "Butes, Steub, Tubes"? Well it was bought by UCSF and will be displayed in the main reception area of the hospital wing."

"They're all really cool," says Jenny. "Beautiful. Each one is sort of abstract in a way."

"Eye sees well, go Weston young woman, formalist you are."

Clare squeezes Ted's thigh lovingly, "Well said, Yoda." They all laugh.

As Kevin approaches the quaint town of Sonoma, Clare says, "There's a public parking lot down one block. We can park there."

When all are out of the car, Clare instructs Kevin, "Why don't you and Jenny stroll around the plaza while I take Ted to see Dr. Kingsley. We'll be through in an hour and will meet you in front of the gallery at three-thirty. OK?"

"Sure, Mom."

Kevin and Jenny hold hands and stroll one way, while Ted and Clare do the same in the opposite direction. Down the block, in front of the Sonoma Bar & Grill, Clare looks at her watch and says, "Right on time. Let's go in."

As they enter the restaurant, Clare is hailed by Dr. Kinsgley, who sits with another fellow in a corner booth. Both gentleman nurse drinks and look as if they've just stepped off a golf course, mainly because they just have.

"Good day, you two. Let me introduce you to Dr. Jim Gates. Jim's a neurologist at UCSF. He's a great doctor and a lousy golfer. That's why we play every weekend."

"Pleased to me you, Dr. Gates. Dr. Kingsley, thanks so much for meeting with us again. Ted seems to be comprehending more and talking more since the last time we saw you."

"Great. Sit down. So, Ted, how are you?" asks Dr. Kingsley.

"Shattered life. On the ground, broken teacups, from another time."

Dr. Gates looks at Ted, then at Clare, then at Dr. Kingsley, and says to Kingsley, "That's interesting. Agrammatic but nicely put."

"The reason I wanted Jim to see Ted is that Jim's an expert on language and thought disorders. Ted's speech is typical of individuals with damage to parts of the frontal lobes. Often patients with frontal lobe damage can only put out brief and somewhat telegraphic speech. Yet Ted's case is most unusual in that he seems to have an unusually colorful way of talking. It's almost as if Ted's perceptions are somewhat disconnected from his thoughts."

Clare remarks, "You know, since his injury we've all noticed his interesting way of describing thoughts and what he sees. I've kept a record of many of his sayings. You know the first thing he said to me after his accident was, 'Cogito ergo alive.'"

"Clever," says Dr. Gates. Turning to Ted, Dr. Gates asks,

"Ted, do you remember much of your hospital stay?"

"Bare trees, rattled by harsh winds, no sound."

"Interestingly put, Ted," responds Dr. Kingsley. "Now I understand why your photography is so beautiful. Yesterday, I visited the gallery. Wonderful work. It doesn't really matter what the objects are that Ted photographs, the patterns of shapes and lines are exquisite. Afterwards I'll take Jim over to the gallery for the reception. Clare, how are things going with you?"

"I've been doing well. My son, Kevin, has been great. He has a nice girlfriend, and he's doing well in school. Ted seems to be coming along. Almost every day we go out somewhere and he does his photography. I read or work on my laptop. I'm on sabbatical leave for the academic year, so we've been having lots of time and fun together. In fact, when I look back and think about our lives before his accident, I sometimes feel that Ted's disposition, his sense about himself, is better than before. He's not so worried or so critical of himself anymore."

"He's what, eight months post-injury? You'll continue to see improvements in his mental abilities. Yet I'm afraid from what we've seen in the scans, full recovery is doubtful," says Dr. Kingsley.

Dr. Gates asks, "How are Ted's motor abilities?"

"He's a little weak on his right side," answers Clare.

Dr. Kingsley holds out his hands and asks Ted, "Ted, reach out and grab my hands."

Ted responds to this request and to several other commands from Dr. Kinglsey. Turning to Dr. Gates, Kinsley says, "Definitely some right-sided weakness as one might expect. The hard part is how to interpret the posterior cortical trauma, how it may have affected perceptual processes." Turning to Ted, Kingsley asks,

"Ted, can you tell us how you think your vision has changed since your accident?"

"Eyes see, thoughts shimmer and trickle by, forms float."

"Sounds like some visual agnosia." Dr. Gates digs into his pants pocket and pulls out his key chain. He shows a key to Ted and asks, "Ted, what's this?"

"Key."

"What's this?"

Key ring."

"What's this?"

"Jaguar. Nice."

"Well, I don't think his basic form perception is off, and his naming is fine. Perhaps it's more conceptual?" Dr. Gates asks Ted, "Ted, do you think your thinking abilities have been affected?"

"Cormorants sit, think about the many fish, that got away."

"You know, that's interesting," says Clare. "That's how he described one of his photographs. It's a beautiful image of two cormorants in the fog. He took it near a beach north of San Francisco a few months ago. You can see it later at the gallery."

Ted smiles.

Dr. Gates turns to Kingsley, "I've really never seen anything like this. I don't know if I'm reading into his utterances more than I should, but the visual associations are stunning. Each response is really poetic, nicely metaphoric, and he certainly seems to comprehend well enough. If I follow what Ted is saying, it appears that his conceptual processes have been compromised, but in its place is a stunning ability to put together visual associations as thoughts."

"Significantly formed. Heightened sensory, memory, emotion. Embodied aesthetics."

"You may not understand that," says Clare. "A while back before his accident, Ted and I talked about a theory of aesthetics that we were working on. He called it, 'embodied aesthetics.' This is the first time he's mentioned it since his injury."

"Very good, Ted," says Dr. Kingsley. "I think you're progressing rather well."

"Yes," confirms Dr. Gates. "I'm very impressed. You're fortunate, Ted, and a remarkable individual."

After a few minutes of chatting with Kingsley and Gates, Clare says, "Thanks so much. We've got to get to the gallery and help set up. Maybe we'll see you at the Inside Out later on?"

"Yes. Always a pleasure to see you two," says Kingsley.

Both Kingsley and Dr. Gates rise from the booth and shake hands with Ted and Clare.

Clare and Ted exit the restaurant and head to the Inside Out. After a short stroll along the plaza, they see Kevin and Jenny sitting on the front steps of the gallery.

"Hey, you two," says Clare.

"Hi, mom."

"Let's go in and see if everything's ready."

Together, they step into the Inside Out and are quickly approached by Eugenia, an earth mother with flowing gray-black hair, earrings larger than donuts, pendulous and braless breasts covered by a colorful tent-sized muumuu, and sandals that appear to have been worn during the Free Speech Movement.

"Hello all," says Eugenia.

"Hello," says Clare, looking around the gallery. "It's lovely in here. You did a wonderful job, Eugenia. We really appreciate your effort and interest."

"My pleasure...Ted, your work is beautiful!" she says, giving

Ted a full-bosomed hug.

Ted nods and smiles. He and Clare stroll around the hall, enjoying the splendor of a roomful of Ted's photographs. Kevin, already munching on some chicken wings, stands with Jenny, admiring the art work.

Eugenia reminds herself, "Oh, I have some friends in the other room who would like to meet you." She turns and heads toward the back door.

Moments later, Eugenia returns with a middle-aged couple, "This is Mary and Max Kohler."

Ted and Clare turn and see Eugenia with a pleasant looking blind woman with dark glasses, who is being led by a thin, well-dressed fellow with a gray, angular goatee.

"Mary had her exhibition here just before yours. She's been blind from birth but has an uncanny sense of color," says Eugenia. "She chooses her colors by taste."

"Yes," says Mary. "I can taste differences in the chemical make-up of paint. I end up mixing all of my colors to taste."

"Good taste...taste good?" asks Ted.

Everyone chuckles.

"Max helps and guides Mary's brushstrokes. It's very interesting watching them work," says Eugenia. "It looks like dancing."

"Yes, it's fun," says Max with a slight German accent. "We really enjoy working together and have been doing so for the past 10 years. I used to paint on my own, but I wasn't very successful."

"And I couldn't do it without Max," says Mary. "Separately we're nothing. Together we make a whole artist!"

Clare smiles, though a little concerned that some may view Ted's exhibition as some kind freak show. She's comforted, however, by the surroundings. On the walls, Ted's work is truly an impressive array of interesting and aesthetically pleasing forms, colors, lines, and curves.

"Oh. Looks like we have some guests arriving," says Eugenia as she ambles toward the front door.

Max, Mary, Ted, and Clare chat next to a table filled with appetizers. Max pours Mary and Clare some white wine, while Ted grabs some sushi from a tray.

"Hey Ted!" Ted turns around and sees Dave Connerly and Leona D'Angelo walking with Eugenia. "Great stuff! Very Brett Weston-like only in color. I'm really impressed!"

Ted blushes, as he receives a kiss from Leona.

As they chat, more visitors enter the gallery, though many are not familiar to Ted or Clare. In fact, some look as if they too are "special" and have had their own showing in Eugenia's gallery. Clare notices Drs. Kingsley and Gates admiring the photo of cormorants that Ted mentioned earlier.

"I think the poems are lovely," says Leona to Clare. "You did a wonderful job setting this up. I imagine it has been a difficult year for you."

"Well, you know, I think this has been my way of coping…of keeping busy. I was just telling the neurologist who sees Ted that in some ways there has been some good in what has happened. You know, he's much calmer and not depressed anymore. We do lots of things together and thank goodness, we don't have financial worries."

"That's really great, Clare. I hope you don't take too personally some of the stuff that's been in the press. They can be vicious. The stuff they say about Ted getting what he deserved is really sick."

"Oh, that doesn't bother me. They're just picking up on the

irony. The performances had to end somehow. I think, ultimately, Ted would have gotten bored and depressed with them. Personally, I think the photography is much more interesting and artistic than his performances."

"Yes, it's funny. The art world wants new and quirky. They don't want beauty. I think Ted's work is lovely, but the art critics would consider his work as passé, representative of early formalist photography."

"I do appreciate your article about Ted a few months ago. It was nice that you included some of his poems."

"My pleasure. I'm so pleased you sent them to me. I love them. Say, why don't you put them all together. Maybe even write a psychological documentary of Ted's life experiences?"

"That's an interesting idea. I have tons of notes on my laptop from our time in the hospital, and I've kept a chronicle of Ted's recovery since we've come home. I'm sure I can work up a biographical sketch of his life before he started blowing things up."

Leona smiles, "Yes. I'll bet the art world would be very interested in a personal biography. You're just the right person to do it."

"You know, just today, for the first time since his accident Ted mentioned 'embodied aesthetics,' a term he made up to describe his new theory of aesthetics. He was hoping that we would write a paper together on the psychology of art and how art has lost its body—its status as a human endeavor. Ted felt that art should excel in expressing our entire psyche: our senses, emotions, and thoughts."

"Sounds interesting. You really should think about writing something up."

Returning home in the afterglow of sunset, Kevin heads up the driveway. Having dropped off Jenny, Kevin is alone in the front with Clare and Ted snuggled close in the back.

"That was really nice," says Clare.

"Yeah, Mom. Thanks for taking me and Jenny and thanks for letting me drive the car. We had a great time. You know, I've really learned a lot from Ted. Not just what he says but also what he did. He really went with his heart on this art stuff, even though he got hurt. But you know, he's getting better, and Jenny thinks he's super. And to think all this happened because I tried to blow up a bomb in front of a 7/11!"

"Don't remind me!" laughs Clare.

"Persimmons hang, restless leaves on broken branch, sweet autumn."

Now alone in the living room, Clare sits on the sofa, laptop on lap and types, "Chapter 1." She pauses for a moment, then begins, "'It's art, but so what?' mumbled Professor Shearing to his semi-conscious class..."

15

Two years later, on page 22 of the *New York Review of Books*, Clare glows as she reads:

The State of the Arts

In her biography of Ted Shearing, the famed conceptual artist, author/psychologist/wife Clare Singer paints a thoughtful picture of Shearing's rise to fame and ultimate fall from a tragic incident. The book, entitled, "Ted Shearing: A Personal Statement of Art," begins with Shearing as a bookish, thirtyish Art History professor working comfortably at a small college in California. Ted diligently lectures to students about art, aesthetics, and criticism, though he garners more fun from his ever developing collection of contemporary art. One day Ted is struck with a depressive epiphany. He judges his own collection as a degradation of what art should be. As a critical statement of contemporary art, he responds with explosives and blowtorch, annihilating pieces in his collection in front of his students. A newspaper article picks up on Ted's performance and, ironically, Shearing himself is heralded as a new force in contemporary art. Spurred by invitations from museums to perform (and having been fired from his academic position for performing), Ted turns his life into a whirlwind of art performances. He enters the art world crowned as the "Anarchist of Art."

Ted's performances ignite enormous interest from the art world as his acts represent an iconoclastic, dare I say "bombastic" approach to artistic expression. Not since Rauschenberg erased a drawing by De Kooning has such blatant disrespect of art been approached. But, on one occasion, a psychopathic copycat artist attempts to ram his car into the entrance of the Los Angeles Modern Art Museum. Fortunately, the crazed driver can't get past Rodin's Balzac who guards the front of the museum. "One of the dangers of modern art," Ted commented to the press—Ted appears to be making a reference to himself and the propriety of his ideas rather than to Balzac or the museum itself.

Meanwhile, another crazed individual, perhaps a disgruntled artist, conceives a plan: kill Ted with a bomb during one of his performances. On the day of a show in New York, a bomb planted in the performance hall explodes on cue. Ted is critically injured and narrowly escapes death. The assailant remains at large, as no one is ever suspected of the attempted murder. Ted has become an enemy of new art, and, as such, his demise could have been promulgated by any of a thousand starving and deranged artists.

Singer portrays Ted as a metaphor for contemporary art. Ted is critic, artist, art destroyer, and in the end someone else's artwork (Singer conceptualizes the plot to murder Ted as a work of art intended by some crazed artist). She promulgates an art theory that she calls "embodied aesthetics," which appears to be based on Ted's views and her own expertise in psychological science. Bottom line: Art can be anything, including reality and its destruction of both the object and the artist. What matters in art? Is contemporary art anything more than a group of elitists deciding which kernels of odd cleverness are worthy?

Where Ted goes, so goes Art. Indeed, as portrayed by Singer, Ted is the embodiment of art itself. So what's the conclusion? Art is Dead? No. Ted is brain damaged. His intellectual skills are impaired, specifically his ability to reflect—to "conceptualize(!)." His brain damage somehow heightens and alters his perceptions. He sees primarily in forms, lines, and colors. He dabbles in photography, using his newfound perception to create interesting images. He speaks in colorful metaphors. He becomes moderately successful as a fine art photographer, though he is completely ignored by the academic art world and is viewed as a once expressively innovative artist, but now a degenerate brain-mushed, hack photographer. He apparently lives happily ever after...

www.ingramcontent.com/pod-product-compliance
Lightning Source LLC
Chambersburg PA
CBHW022026170626
46808CB00003B/1078